Eliza

Annie Seaton

Pentecost Island 2

ISBN 978-0-6487948-6-8

DEDICATION

*To the wonderful girlfriends
I have made through my writing... author and
readers alike!*

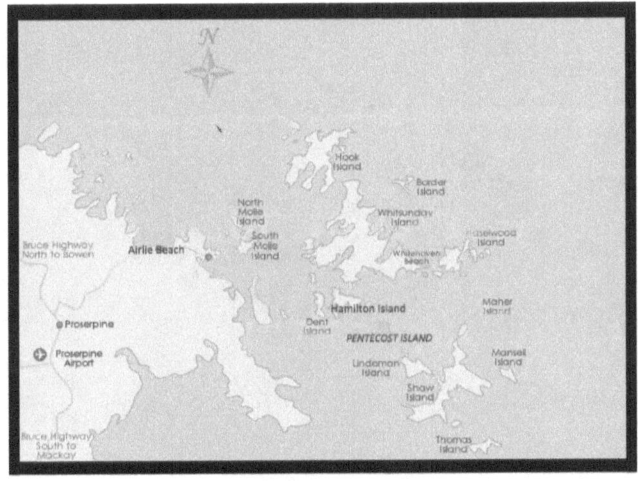

WHITSUNDAY ISLANDS

Prologue
Pippa: Pentecost Island

A bottle of bubbles didn't last long between four when there was a celebration underway. The floors of the first four huts had been laid today, and now we were ready to put up the modular buildings. The frames were stacked waiting for us to begin work tomorrow.

I lifted my glass in a toast. 'To Ma Carmichael's Place.'

'To Ma's,' my three friends chimed in.

We clinked glasses and sipped at our champagne.

We were sitting on the sand looking across the bay to the peak that marked the centre of the island. Evie and Nell had gone for a quick swim while they'd waited for Tam and I to come down with the bubbles and the glasses. The sun was warm as spring approached and we all wore our straw hats.

'I think, ladies, when we get the interiors of the huts done, we might set an opening date and work towards that. What do you think of that?'

'Super,' Nell said.

Tam giggled. 'You're getting an English accent too. Or the lingo, at least.'

Nell nudged her and Tam's glass tipped a little.

'Hey, watch it, I'll spill my bubbles!'

Evie laughed with them. 'It's just like being back at uni, being here on the island with you lot. No cares, no worries, no pressure.'

I rolled my eyes. 'No, just a resort under development, a huge landscaping project'—I nodded at Evie— 'and a huge accounting task underway, thanks to Nell, and an outdoor restaurant and menus to be planned.' I raised my glass. 'Thank you, all.'

'That's right.' Tam nodded. 'Just like Evie said. No cares, no worries, no pressure.'

'And let's keep it that way. I want to propose another toast.' I lifted my glass. 'To friendship, girls. To the unbreakable bond that has seen us stay together through the ups and downs of life. And boy, there's been some of them over the past ten years.'

'To friendship,' they chorused.

As the sun slipped slowly towards the sea, we sat there in silence. Four women who cared for and looked out for each other. When the bubbles were finished, we put our glasses down and looped our arms around each other's shoulders. The sky faded from that deep indigo blue into an array of pinks shot with gold, and the only sound was the small waves breaking on the shingly sand.

I smiled as a light came on up the hill and Rafe's silhouette appeared at the window as he looked down to the bay.

Our bay.

He wouldn't be able to see us, but I could see him. I was beside Tam and I felt her tense as she leaned forward.

'Pip, what's that?'

I pulled my gaze away from Rafe's house and looked in the direction she was pointing. 'What?'

'There's something in the water. Look just

out at the point. Something black.'

'A shark?' Nell shuddered. 'We were just swimming out there before you came down.'

'No.' Tam jumped to her feet and we watched as she ran down to the water.

I stood and held out my hand to pull Nell up.

'I think it's a person,' Tam called back to us. 'I'm going to go out to the point.'

It was too dark to see clearly, and I couldn't imagine that Tam was right. There were no boats in sight, and no lights, unless there was a boat around the point in Back Bay. Even so it was too late at night for someone to be in the water. I wouldn't even swim in the daytime; I was worried about the shark attacks a couple of years ago and was very wary.

When the business could afford it, I intended to put a pool in, adjacent to the outdoor restaurant.

And a jacuzzi, and a day spa. My thoughts went into planning mode as we followed Tam out onto the rocky point. It was too dark to see, but the closer we got to the water, the more I could hear splashing in the water.

'Could be dolphins,' I said.

Tam yelled as we were almost to her. 'It's a person, and I think they're in trouble.' As we took off towards her, she threw her hat to the ground, pulled her dress over her head and stepped into the water. Before we could reach her, she was swimming out into the bay.

'Tam, don't be stupid,' I yelled.

I looked around quickly. We were at the opposite end of the bay to the jetty, and by the time I could run over and start the launch, she could be back in.

But nevertheless, I remained poised to run as Nell picked up Tam's dress and hat.

I stared at the water and it was only a minute or two later that the splashing reached us followed by Tam's voice. She sounded out of breath.

'I've got them. I'll swim into the beach. It'll be easier than getting out on the rocks.'

I half held my breath as we raced around to the beach and waited for Tam to appear. By the time we got there I was breathless, and Nell was close to tears.

'Oh, Pip, is she going to make it?' she cried.

Gradually we could make out a disturbance in the water and I prayed under my breath that she would get in safely.

Suddenly there was a huge splash, and Tam appeared in front of us. She was dragging a person by the armpits and we all hurried into the water to help her.

It was a woman. She was wearing a long white dress and it clung to her legs, impeding her progress. We each put our hands beneath her and carried her into the shore.

'Are you okay, Tam?' I glanced over at my brave friend. I was in awe of her bravery. There was no way I could have done that.

'I'm fine. I think she is too. She was swimming by herself, but I think she passed out when I reached her.

We lay the woman on her side in the recovery position, and I was relieved when she coughed and groaned. It was almost too dark to see.

'Evie, Nell, run up to the house and get a blanket and some water,' I said as I bent down with

Tam.

The woman was breathing on her own, and as I watched her eyes flickered open.

'Thank you,' she whispered.

'Are you all right? Can you breathe okay? Are you hurt anywhere?' Tam fired questions at her, and the woman nodded.

'I'm okay. Thank you.' Her voice was stronger, and she tried to sit up. 'Please help me sit up, it'll be easier to catch my breath.'

Her voice had a slight accent that I couldn't place, and her dark hair was plastered to her skull in wet ringlets. Her eyes were dark and wide.

Tam and I supported her as she sat up on the sand.

'What's your name?' I asked.

'Eliza.' Her voice was faint.

'How did you get in the water?' Tam asked.

She looked us both blankly. 'I don't know.'

Chapter 1
Marissa: Florence, Italy 2018

'Marissa Meynell! You have not changed one bit!'

Marissa looked up at her best friend with a grin and carefully stroked the last layer of pale pink nail polish onto her fingernails. The huge diamond on her left hand glinted as she moved her hand. She screwed the cap onto the tiny bottle and placed it on the table near the large metal door. 'What do you mean, I haven't changed?'

Sienna stood there, hands on hips and tapping her foot on the marble floor, her elegant brows drawn together in a frown. 'I mean it's your wedding day, we're about to be picked up'—she reached down and smoothed an invisible crease from the pretty mauve silk sheath dress that Rosco had insisted on paying for—'and you only started getting ready fifteen minutes ago and now you're painting your nails!'

'But I do look okay, don't I?' For a minute a niggle of worry flared in Marissa's stomach. The contrast with her best friend's appearance had always been obvious. Sienna had even managed to look elegant and well-groomed as she'd scooted down the hockey field at their boarding school in Kent where they'd become best friends fifteen years ago.

Marissa always managed to look crumpled and untidy. Her idea of comfort was a pair of jeans and a T-shirt, and her long curly hair pulled back in a braid. A hasty dab of lip gloss on her way out the door was her usual method of wearing makeup. She'd gone blonde when she was eighteen thinking it would help her look more elegant, but it was just a pain getting the regrowth done. But she persevered; they said blondes had more fun, and she was proving them right.

Her complete opposite, Sienna always looked perfect no matter what time of day it was. Her glossy auburn hair fell in a perfect bob that brushed her long graceful neck, and her makeup was always meticulously applied. She'd started getting ready for the wedding about two hours ago, while Marissa had roamed around the apartment wondering if she was doing the right thing.

'You look gorgeous.' Sienna reached out and tucked a stray blonde curl behind Marissa's ear. 'As you always do. If I could look like you do without the effort I have to put in, I would be one very happy woman.'

Marissa reached up and touched the blonde curls that she had tried to smooth into a semblance of order. 'The girls at uni always called me Barbie because of my thick blonde hair.' She chuckled as she looked down at the high-necked wedding dress. 'But I certainly missed out in the Barbie boob department,' she said putting on an American accent. She was a natural mimic and going to school with girls from all over the world had given her a repertoire of accents.

Sienna smiled back at her. 'You look stunning, so stop worrying. I'd much rather be a blue-eyed blonde with your olive skin than red-haired and green eyed and a lily-white complexion.'

Their conversation was interrupted by a loud

jingling and Marissa's mouth dropped open.

'*Bella?* Are you all right?' Sienna held her hand out. 'Come on, your carriage awaits.'

Marissa nodded as she put one hand to her lips and took Sienna's outstretched hand with the other.

'Oh, my goodness. Look at that. Surely that can't be for us, Sienna. Can it? I really hope it's not.'

'I don't see any other brides here waiting for transport.' Sienna Marino squeezed Marissa's fingers and pulled a face. 'Sorry, but your Rosco swore me to secrecy.'

Marissa shook her head and leaned back against the heavy metal door in the carriageway beneath the apartment where the girls had been staying for the past week. The horse and carriage came to a stop beside them.

'Careful.' Sienna tugged Marissa's fingers and pulled her away from the door. 'You will mark your wedding dress.' As well as having spent a week in a fifteenth century palace that was now a modern apartment, Sienna's lilting accent was another reminder to Marissa that they were in Italy, and that her best friend from Switzerland was about to be her bridesmaid.

At *her* wedding. To a man she had met six weeks ago. But, oh what a wonderful man. Not only did Rosco Bertolini have movie star looks—"George Clooney" was often whispered around them as they'd walked the streets of Florence over the past month—and a movie star name, but he was also kind and generous and as madly in love with her as she was with him.

It was like a dream . . . or a fairy tale. Six

weeks ago, Marissa had been a chippie on a work crew in east London, saving for her dream holiday to Italy.

Today she was marrying the man of her dreams; the man she had fallen in love with the moment she had seen him sitting by the river Arno watching the wooden tourist boats go by. She'd never believed in love at first sight, but her attention had been caught by the billowing white shirt he wore, and the jet-black hair that gleamed in the late afternoon sun.

She'd nudged Sienna. 'Why is it that Italian men are so much better looking than men at home?' Look at that gorgeous specimen,' she whispered as she kept her eyes on him as they had drifted past in the flat-bottomed *barchetti*. It might have been the Tuscan rosé she was sipping that gave Marissa a confidence that was out of character, but she had lifted her glass in a salute to the guy as they had floated past.

When he had been waiting at the wharf when they disembarked, she had been embarrassed and surprised, but . . . flattered. Rosco stood there holding out two glasses of champagne.

'Welcome to Florence.' His voice had matched the rest of him. 'May I take you both for dinner?' His eyes had held Marissa's and heat had rushed to her face. He was even better looking close up, but a little older than she'd first thought.

She had looked at Sienna and her friend had shrugged.

'Why not?' They'd exchanged a glance; their budget was tight, so the offer of dinner was one to jump at.

That first night Rosco had taken them to a

cute little restaurant in an alleyway near the Uffizi Gallery, and Marissa had not been able to take her eyes from his gorgeous face as he'd treated them to a magnificent dinner. His deep melodious voice had kept her hanging off his every word all night as she'd watched his full lips smile back at her. His eyes were dark and held hers in their depths as they'd eaten their way through five courses—*primo, secondo,* pasta and pizza, a main course and then *tiramisu* to die for—as well as drinking a considerable quantity of fine Italian wine, and then *limoncello*.

'Come on.' Sienna's voice intruded on her thoughts. 'If you're sure you're going to do this, it's time.'

With a gentle sigh Marissa looked down at the beautiful white silk dress that caressed her legs in the slight breeze that was blowing in from the *Via dei Serragli.* She felt like pinching herself. The fabric had come from an exclusive fashion house in Florence where Rosco had insisted on paying for her wedding dress.

Not only had he paid for it, but he had chosen the design, as well as the gorgeous soft handmade leather shoes she wore. She had protested and he had waved a dismissive hand. 'It is for my beautiful wife-to-be, and *cara mia,* we will only have one wedding, so I want you to be perfect. Wait until you see the beautiful silk nightgown I have bought for our wedding night. It will match your gorgeous blue eyes.'

The usual dry retort that the old Marissa would have made, disappeared along with many of her London habits as she had fallen under Rosco's spell more and more every day.

For a moment, she had considered protesting; it would have been nice if she'd had some say in the wedding, her clothes, and the organisation of the day, but Rosco had planned everything, and she didn't want to take away from his excitement. It was enough for her that he wanted to marry her.

'Marissa. It's not too late.' Sienna's fingers squeezed hers.

'Too late for what?'

'To change your mind and come back to London with me and think about this a bit longer. I will be there for a few months until I go home.'

'Why would I change my mind?' She stared at Sienna. 'I love Rosco.'

'I know. And he loves you. But perhaps there is no need to marry quite so quickly. You could take more time to get to know each other more.'

'No one has ever loved me like he does.' Marissa shook her head. 'I have never been so sure of anything in my life.'

The second night Sienna had met up with some Italian friends and Rosco had taken Marissa to dinner—alone—and . . .

'Come on then. If you are sure, you don't want to be late.' Sienna tugged at her hand again.

'No, I don't.' They were expected at the *Palazza Vecchio* at noon.

'We will have a civil wedding, my darling. I know you are not Roman Catholic yet, so I have booked the *Sala Rossa*. We can look at your conversion before we have children,' Rosco had said.

Marissa had opened her mouth to protest at

that statement; her family had been Church of England since the Reformation, and she had no intention of embracing a new religion, but Rosco had pulled her into his arms and silenced her with a kiss.

'I cannot wait until you see the palace on our wedding day,' he said, his lips warm and soft against hers. 'The opulent furnishings and beautiful frescoes, and the masterpieces that line the walls make it a place of beauty that will give us a wonderful start to our life together.'

If she'd looked more closely then, perhaps she would have seen the unusual intensity and determination in his eyes. But today on her wedding day, excitement and anticipation tingled from her fingertips to every nerve ending in her body.

'Marissa!'

She turned from her introspection as Sienna tugged again. 'The *fiaccheraio* is waiting for us.'

'The what?'

A tall man with silver hair held his hand out to her.

'The carriage driver,' Sienna said with a giggle. 'I look forward to your grasp of the language improving very quickly when you are married to an Italian.'

'I'm not happy about the carriage at all,' Marissa whispered. 'I saw the demonstration in the square the other day, where they were drawing attention to the heat and the conditions that these poor horses have to work in. I would prefer to get a taxi. If I'd known that Rosco was going to organise this, I would have put my foot down.'

'No, no, no.' The carriage driver shook his head emphatically and pointed to his chest. 'Me, I follow the rules. I love my horse and I would not put him in any way of the harm.'

Marissa reluctantly let the man assist her into the carriage, and when she was settled on the burgundy velvet seat, Sienna followed and passed her one of the red rose bouquets that had been waiting in the foyer when they had come down from the apartment.

The ride to the *palazza* through cool and narrow side streets shaded by medieval buildings eased some of the guilt caused by riding in the horse drawn carriage. Tourists waved to them and called out as the horse clopped his way along the cobblestones.

But if she'd had her way, she still wouldn't have condoned it.

'Get the glum look from your face. We are almost there, and the photographers will be waiting.' Sienna squeezed her hand again. 'You're sure you're not getting cold feet, are you?'

Was that a glimmer of hope in Sienna's voice?

'No, of course not.' Joy filled Marissa's chest and she buried her face in the sweet-smelling roses. 'I am excited and honoured to be marrying the man I love.'

'Do you mind that your family could not make it?'

'No. We'll see them soon.' The guilt rushed back, and heat crept up Marissa's neck. Although she had told Sienna her family couldn't attend, they were unaware that she was marrying Rosco today. Sienna was the only one who knew.

Mother would be ecstatic that she was marrying into the Italian aristocracy, not to mention wealth. Marissa knew she was a disappointment to her parents with the life she led, and the profession she had chosen. She had never felt loved by them since she was a child. Her two sisters seemed to be what her parents had wanted in children, but Marissa—the third daughter—was very different to her siblings.

'A what?' Her mother's voice echoed in her thoughts.

'A chippy.' Marissa had stood in front of her mother in the hall of their thirteenth century manor, hands on hips, staring down at her work boots. Boots and socks that certainly looked out of place on the huge black and white chequered tiles of this elegant, but tired manor house.

'You are turning away a position in your father's company to be a common labourer? A position in the family company that has been an institution in this family for over two hundred years?' Mother's voice had been shrill.

'I am an artisan, Mother, not a labourer. Our first job is restoring the timberwork on a shopfront in the Royal Arcade off Old Bond Street.' Marissa had quickly regretted trying to upset her mother by referring to her job as a chippy. 'A craftsperson. That should appeal to your sensibilities.'

One last sniff and Mother had disappeared up the stairs.

Nevertheless, Marissa had suggested to Rosco that they invite her parents to Florence for the wedding, but he had talked her out of it, and she hadn't pushed it.

'Let's surprise them with a visit. We can get your new wardrobe in Paris, and I'm sure your mother will be delighted to see you in designer labels, from what you have told me about her.'

Perhaps Mother might be delighted, but Marissa was tempted to say she was happy with her current wardrobe. But spoiling her seemed to give Rosco pleasure too, and he assured her over and over that he could afford it.

'We will visit your Meynell Manor in Derbyshire on our honeymoon, and I will meet your family. I am nervous that they will not like me. I do not want them to change your mind before you become my wife.' Rosco's voice had been uncertain as he held her.

Marissa had hugged him. 'I will not change my mind.'

It was only a small white lie she had told Sienna.

A lie that would come back to haunt her.

Six months later, Marissa was to wonder what had happened to her in those six delirious weeks. Forty-two whirlwind days that had eventuated in her marrying a man twenty years older than her.

Chapter 2
Pippa: Pentecost Island

Current day

Evie and Nell didn't take long to come back from the house with a bottle of water, a blanket and a thick towel. Tam and I were sitting beside the dark-haired woman on the sand. It wasn't too cool in the late winter evening, but she was shivering as though it was the middle of winter.

'Thanks.' Tam removed her arm from the woman's shoulder and took the towel that Nell held out as Evie popped the top off the water bottle.

'A drink of water first, and then we'll get that wet dress off you,' Evie said calmly.

How the hell the woman called Eliza had managed to swim in that long dress and not drown was beyond me. It was easy to see that she wore a pair of black swimmers beneath the white dress that was clinging to her wet legs.

She said couldn't remember how she came to be in the water, but she couldn't have come far. She had to have come off a boat because the closest island was Little Lindeman Island to the south and that was over two kilometres away. Too far to swim to our island.

As Tam helped peel off the wet dress with Nell's help, I gestured for Evie to walk along the beach with me.

'Can you jump in your tender and go for a bit of a scoot around to Back Bay. She has to have come off a boat.'

'Maybe she fell overboard and hit her head?' Evie said quietly with a glance back up the beach. 'Seems strange that she can't remember how she got in the water. Have you checked her eyes?'

'Not yet,' I said. 'Keeping her warm was our first priority. I think she's in shock.'

'If she'd hit her head she would've gone under and not appeared at the front of our bay.' Evie's voice was still quiet. 'Someone must be out there looking for her. I'll go out now and look for a boat.'

I nodded and went back to the group on the beach as Evie headed towards the wharf at the base of the hill beneath Rafe's house.

I tapped my finger on my lips as I stared up at his house on the hill; the lights glowed softly as the dark surrounded us on the beach. I wondered for a moment if I should go up and tell him what had happened, and then realised there was nothing he could do.

Besides, he'd be working. Rafe was editing his new book and had it almost ready to send back to his publisher in London.

'Pip?' Tam's voice drew me over. 'Eliza is feeling a little better now. I think we should go up to the house.'

'Thank you for the water. My legs have stopped shaking now. I should be able to stand up.' This time there was no accent to her words.

Tam and Nell took an arm each and helped Eliza to her feet. I stood in front of them in case she fainted or anything.

'Do you remember your last name,' I asked quietly as she stood gripping the girls' hands.

She nodded. 'Pengelly. I am Eliza Pengelly.'

'Your address?'

This time a frown and her words were hesitant. 'Um. I don't have a current one. I used to live in Brisbane. At the Gap. But I don't live there anymore.'

'So where do you live now?'

'I'm on a holiday. A working holiday' Her voice was soft and there was just enough light for me to see her close her eyes. 'I remember now. I was on my kayak.'

Tam and I exchanged a glance.

On a kayak? In a long white dress with no lifejacket? It didn't ring true for me.

'You weren't wearing a life jacket then?' Tam asked echoing my thoughts

She shook her head. 'No, but I had been. I'd been out fishing in my kayak and when I caught enough, I went back to the island. Um, Dylan was going to get the fire going and cook them and he asked me to go to the other end of the beach to collect some firewood. That's why I was wearing a dress. I was only paddling to the end of the beach.'

'Which island?' Nell asked quietly. She had more patience that Tam and I did with the changing answers.

Eliza frowned and let go of Tam's hand and pressed her fingers to her forehead. Her short dark curls were plastered to her forehead. 'Little something I think Dylan said.'

'Little Lindeman?' I asked.

She nodded and dropped her hand. 'Yes, that was it. I've been there a few days. I joined a group.'

'A group?' Tam took her arm again.

'Dylan, Alex and Marissa. There were more,

but they left when the boat came.' Her voice was getting stronger now and again there was that twang of an accent.

Maybe Kiwi, I thought.

'Oh my God, they'll think I drowned.' Confusion crossed her face as she put her hand to her head again.

'Did they see you get in the kayak? Do you know any of their mobile numbers?' I peppered her with questions. 'We could call and say you've turned up here,' I said.

Nell flicked me a glance and shook her head. 'I think before we do any of that we need to get Eliza up to the house, and into a hot shower.'

'Yes. we do. Come on. We'll help you along.' Tam's voice was brisk as she led the dark-haired woman up the beach.

I followed, a frown on my face, still wondering how and why she ended up on our island.

Something didn't feel right for me.

Chapter 3

Marissa

'Dubrovnik? I thought we were flying to Paris, and then England?' Marissa frowned as she looked down at the boarding pass that Rosco handed her at Roma International Airport the afternoon after their wedding. 'To see my family?'

They had taken the train from Florence in a first-class carriage mid-morning, and a hire car had been waiting to whisk them straight to the airport.

Rosco moved his head lower and his breath whispered along her neck. 'We are, my love, but first we are going to have a week alone on my yacht. Just you and me.'

'*Your* yacht?' Marissa widened her eyes.

My God, who is this man?

'Yes, my other beautiful lady. My *Lady Calypso.* I wanted to have some time alone with you in a beautiful place before we head to that cold and rainy island you used to call home.'

'Perhaps you could have told me your plans.' Marissa stiffened and moved away from his hold, but Rosco's fingers tightened on her arm.

'It was going to be a surprise, *cara mia.*' His face fell and Marissa reached up to brush her lips across her husband's cheek. 'It is going to be a honeymoon that any woman would want.'

'I'm sorry for snapping, darling. It sounds wonderful but perhaps next time you could tell me if there is a change of plans?'

His lips tightened. 'We are going to the Adriatic Sea and I am showing you my favourite place in the whole world. I have never taken a woman there before. Do you know how special that is?'

Even though his words made her feel a little uncomfortable, Marissa smiled as she wondered how many women he *had* taken to other places. She was being silly. At forty-two and an eligible bachelor, she had to accept that of course there had been women in Rosco's life before he had fallen in love with her. *She* was the inexperienced one.

Inexperienced with men, love and this whole relationship thing.

Gosh, no. This *marriage* thing. A cold feeling shimmied down her back, and she bit down the anxiety that tugged at her.

'Where is this place?' Her voice was calm, and she was pleased it didn't reflect that nerves were taking hold.

'It is an easy sail off the coast of Dubrovnik. The island of Mljet.' The word rolled off Rosco's tongue and his sexy accent sent a luscious shiver down her spine. 'Legend has it that Mljet is the island of Ogygia where the nymph, Calypso, kept the Greek hero, Odysseus, captive for seven years. The ancient name for the island is Melitta, which comes from the Greek *melitte nesos*.'

'What does that mean?'

Even though they were in full view of the other passengers waiting to board, Rosco's lips settled on her neck. 'It means honey island. Perhaps you will want to keep me captive there like Odysseus' nymph did.'

'Did he escape?' she whispered back as his lips crept up her neck.

'He did. Even though she promised him

immortality if he stayed with her.'

Marissa swayed as her legs trembled when her husband of twenty-four hours nipped the lobe of her ear. Pulling back, she shook her head as a blush warmed her cheeks. 'Please wait until we get to our room.'

The island of Mljet was everything that Rosco had promised . . . and more. Marissa sighed as he dropped the main sail of *Lady Calypso* and it came down quickly into the sail bag. Everything happened quickly on this boat, and she had hidden her trepidation every time the boat had leaned over as they had sailed up the coast from Dubrovnik. Her experience on the sea was non-existent.

Although in one way she was pleased to learn that there were no other crew on Rosco's boat, she had learned how to help and what ropes to hold over the past day. Rosco said the sea had been smooth as they had sailed across a wide expanse of water with no land in sight.

'You look worried.'

She jumped as he came up behind her, his white-soled shoes making no noise on the timber deck.

'I'm still not used to being on board a boat that tips over with every wave and puff of wind.' The wind had picked up and was blowing quite strongly as they got closer to the rocky foreshore of the island. 'I'm embarrassed to admit it, but the only other time I've been on a boat was on the ferry from Calais to Dover on a school excursion.'

Rosco raised his eyebrows, but his smile was encouraging, even though his words came as a surprise. 'You will soon get used to living on the sea. If the wind stays like this, we will have some excellent sailing days.'

'How long did you say we would be on the boat?'

'I was thinking a week, but I have had an excellent idea. If the wind stays up like this, we could sail around Italy to the *Cote d'Azur* and fly to Paris from Nice.'

'How long would that take?' Marissa frowned, not sure how she felt about spending more than few days living on this yacht.

'Don't you want to have a long honeymoon with me?' Rosco pulled her closer. She shivered as his hand ran down her back and lingered at the top of her shorts. 'When we travel—and we will travel most of the year, *Lady Calypso*—or my motor cruiser, *Nymph*—will take us where we want to go. And quickly.'

'Oh. Your motor cruiser?'

'Smile, my darling.' Rosco tapped a finger on her cheek as he let her go. 'Once we motor into the bay and drop the anchor it will be calm. I don't want a wife who is afraid.'

Marissa responded with a smile, despite her stomach feeling as though her lunch may not stay there. 'I'm fine.' She spread her arms wide. 'And look how beautiful it is here.' She watched as Rosco went back to the helm, and a ripple of pleasure and anticipation of the nights ahead filled her with excitement.

Her wedding night had surpassed all expectations. Rosco had insisting on waiting until they were married, and he had been a gentle and considerate lover; even listening to his deep voice now brought a shiver to her skin. Seven days alone in a boat would be wonderful, but no more than that this trip. He had promised when they didn't invite her parents to the wedding, that they would go to England and tell them in person. It didn't matter if she didn't get home to see her family for at least another two weeks. She wasn't due home from her Italian holiday until then, so they wouldn't worry. She would give them a call later—just to touch base—not to tell them she was married and on her honeymoon.

'Shit.' For the first time, reality tugged at Marissa, and a strange feeling settled in her stomach. With those words at the ceremony, her life had changed and irrevocably set her on a new path.

It didn't matter what her family thought. And it didn't matter that she wouldn't go back to her job in London—she'd hated the city anyway—she had made a commitment.

A lifelong commitment. Her fingers fluttered with nerves and she swallowed.

But Rosco turned to her, and her doubts dissolved instantly as his lips tilted in a smile. He lifted his fingers and blew her a kiss before he took the helm

Marissa kept her eyes on him as he steered the boat through a narrow channel into a protected cove. Thick luxuriant pine woods tumbled down to the shoreline, and the pungent smell of cypress carried across on the breeze. She breathed a sigh of relief once the anchor was over and the boat stopped rocking.

'Don't worry, I have set the anchor firmly

and we have forty metres of chain holding us steady.'

Her grin was cheeky. 'That means nothing to me.'

'What it means is we won't be going anywhere.'

'Will we be eating on the boat? Or is there a restaurant that we can go to?'

Rosco's laugh blew away on the stiff wind as he stood up from the anchor bay. 'If you would like to walk four miles there is a delightful little restaurant in a small village over the cliffs. We will go there one night, but tonight I have other plans.'

'Other plans? She swallowed and her legs trembled as his smile widened.

'I think we shall strip off and cool down with a swim, and then I will lie on the deck while you cook my dinner.'

'Oh, will you?' Marissa swallowed nervously again. She hadn't told Rosco that cooking was something she had little experience with. Let alone cooking in the tiny little galley that held a small gas stove and a tiny sink.

She hadn't thought about food when he had stocked the boat assuming that they would eat out every night.

'Um, I'll just go down and get my bikini on.'

He shook his head and his smile was almost predatory. 'You won't need your bikini.' He held her gaze as he undid the tie on his white shorts and dropped them to the deck.

Oh my God.

He was naked.

And beautiful.

Marissa's husband walked over and lifted her T-shirt over her head, and within seconds her state of dress matched his.

His lips ran down her neck and desire flared as one hand cupped her breast. 'Perhaps we will swim later, my dear.'

Chapter 4

Pippa

I went back to collect the empty wine bottle and glasses from the beach while Nell sorted towels for Eliza in the bathroom and hovered outside as she took a shower. Tam got a meal underway, and soon the usual aromatic smells were coming from the kitchen she had now made her own.

I was sad our celebration had been interrupted by the arrival of this mystery woman, but at the same time I was pleased she had swum to our bay instead of meeting an untimely end somewhere out in those waters.

As I bent down to pick up the glasses, the sound of a motor reached me. I straightened and put my hand to my eyes and squinted in the darkness. A small light shone across the water near the end of the wharf as Evie motored towards it. There was something behind her rubber tender, but I couldn't make out what it was.

I hurried along the beach and ran up the three stairs to the wharf.

'Pippa?' Rafe's voice called from above me. I paused and waited until he came down the steps on the hill and jumped down onto the wharf beside me.

'Hello.' His arms went around me, and his warm lips took mine before I could say a word. I hugged him back and then pulled away when Evie's tender bumped the end of the wharf.

'Is everything okay?' he asked. 'I saw you all on the beach and the tender go out before.'

'We've had a bit of drama tonight,' I said tugging at his hand as I moved to the end of the wharf.

Evie was still in the tender and I could see a light shape was floating beside the rubber boat.

'Drama?' he asked.

'Yes, a woman was in trouble swimming around the point and we got her onto the shore. Evie went out looking for a boat. Tam and Nell are up at the house with her.'

'Is she all right?' His hand still held mine.

'Seems to be, but we were worried that someone was out there looking for her. She said she was on a kayak. It's too far for anyone to swim from any of the islands.'

'Found it,' Evie called up from the tender. 'This was floating around the point. She must have got caught in the rough waves at the front of Back Bay.

Back Bay was notorious for irregular tidal eddies in contrary wind and tide conditions. For the unwary sailor, it was easy for a yacht to get into trouble, let alone a kayak. Experienced sailors knew to stay to the starboard side when coming out into the channel, and not risk the conditions when the channel opening met swirling eddies.

I frowned. 'She reckons she was over on Little Lindeman.'

'Has to be hers,' Evie said. 'I couldn't see any mast lights out there. And I found this in the cavity.' As she climbed out of the tender, she held up a waterproof bag.

Rafe dropped my hand and moved over to where Evie now stood. 'Do you want me to bring that kayak up onto the wharf?'

I nodded. 'Good idea. The wind seems to be picking up, and the last thing we want is for it to float out to the channel and create a hazard for any boats out there tonight.'

Evie handed me the waterproof bag and went to help Rafe. They each lifted an end of the kayak and soon it was on the wharf.

It was almost pitch dark and Evie reached into the tender for a flashlight. She switched it on, and I could see the contents of the clear bag I was holding.

'There's a couple of envelopes in here,' I said.

'Should we look or give it to her?' Evie asked.

'Let me think about it while you two bring the kayak over to the beach. We'll put it under the trees behind the huts.'

I followed Evie and Rafe as they carried the old kayak off the wharf and along our beach. I wasn't sure what to do.

My good old "spidey" sense had kicked in, and I had a bad feeling about our visitor. Well, not bad, I suppose. Just a feeling things weren't as they seemed. I don't mean that we were all going to be murdered in our beds by some madwoman, but I just found it hard to believe that she would conveniently get into trouble in the water right where the four of us happened to be sitting on a beach, and close enough to rescue her easily. But I couldn't think of any logical explanation for it, other than what she'd said. I'd be grilling her later tonight.

'I can hear your brain whirring away,' Rafe said when they put the kayak down and joined me where I waited at the track.

I chuckled. 'I've been spending too much time with you, Mr Author. My imagination is in overdrive.'

'Not spending enough time with me, to my mind,' he said as he caught my hand.

A rush of pleasure ran through me. I don't think I've ever been happier than I've been since Tam and Nell and I came to Pentecost Island.

Our new resort—*Ma Carmichael's Place*—was taking shape, Evie had joined us, and the gardens were already looking better. The first huts were about to go up and our plans to open for business in three months were on track.

I found myself waking up with a smile most days, and the happiness stayed with me all day. There'd been no dark moments for weeks, and I was sure that the sadness that had been a part of me for so much of my life had gone. Since Aunty Vi had left me her island—well, half of it, Rafe owned the other half—I had begun to heal and look at the world in a very different way.

And I was lucky enough to have the best girlfriends as part of my life—and part of my business project.

And then there was Rafe.

I was trying to go slow. We'd had a rocky start, but he was now a very big part of my happiness. If I was honest, I would say he was more than a big part. I knew if he moved away from our island, I would be devastated.

He wanted to move faster, but with my past track record, I needed to take it slowly, and God love him, he said he would agree to any terms I offered.

'What do you think about the bag?' Evie asked. 'Is it breaching her privacy if we open it?'

'Well, we really don't know that the kayak is Eliza's, do we? She said she was in a kayak, so I guess we could look in to see if it's hers. There are clues in those envelopes.' I turned to Rafe. 'Do you think that's a fair call?'

'I do. You've rescued a woman from drowning and salvaged an unattended kayak. If there is a connection you'll hopefully find out, and it might shed light on how she got to the island.'

'Evie, can you shine the light here please,' I asked as I held the sealed bag up.

She obliged and Rafe stood close to me as I unclipped the Ziplock waterproof bag and tipped the two envelopes into my hand.

I handed the thicker one to Rafe to hold and I lifted the flap on the thinner envelope and turned it over. A small black booklet fell into my hand. Before I opened it, I shook the envelope but there was nothing else inside.

'It looks like a passport,' Evie commented.

I opened the booklet, and sure enough it was a New Zealand-issued passport. Rafe's breath brushed my cheek as he leaned forward.

'What name is in it?'

I turned to the second page and a photo of the woman Tam had rescued stared back at me. She was a very pretty woman, her blue eyes fringed by thick dark lashes—the sort of lashes I had attempted to achieve with all sorts of mascara when I was working—and her cheeks glowing a healthy pink. I scanned the printed details.

'Yep. What she said. Eliza Pengelly and her address says Krage Place, at the Gap in Brisbane.'

'She's thinner in that photograph,' Evie commented. 'Not that she's big now, but she was very thin then. What date is the passport?'

I looked at the bottom line. 'It's a newish one. Valid until 2029.'

Rafe held the other envelope out. 'I think you need to look in here. By the feel of it, I can guess what's in there.'

I looked up at him curiously and his expression was hard to read as I held his gaze. I took the envelope from him and slid my finger beneath the flap.

My mouth dropped open as I peered in. 'Holy fuck.'

'Money?' he asked.

'*And* jewellery.' I nodded and Evie peered over my shoulder.

'Wow. A shitload of money,' she said.

'And what looks like a diamond ring.' I bit my bottom lip and looked back at Rafe. 'There must be a few thousand dollars in there. All in one hundred-dollar notes. Why would someone be in a kayak with a passport and carrying so much money and diamonds?'

'And wearing a dress out kayaking?' Evie added. 'It's bizarre.'

'What do you think we should do?' I put the passport back into its envelope and then slid both envelopes back into the Ziplock bag. 'Should we tell her we found her kayak? And the envelopes? Or should we find out more about her before we do?'

'You think they might not be hers?' Rafe asked.

'I guess they are. It's her photo, and a passport is an authentic form of identification, isn't it?' I shrugged. 'I guess we go back to the house, see how she is and tell her we found the kayak.'

Evie stared down at the envelopes. 'If she thinks the kayak is lost, she'll be pretty damned upset. Losing all that money and passport.'

'The whole situation has me intrigued. Is it all right if I come with you?' Rafe put his arm around me. I leaned into the hard angles of his body, the feel of his skin and the smell of his woody aftershave were becoming very familiar to me, and I liked that.

'Of course. I think you should join us for dinner. Tam was making a huge pot of curry when we left.' I narrowed my eyes. 'You can be the observer and tell us what you think of our mermaid.'

By the time we'd walked up to the house, Evie's comment turned into an accurate prediction. A loud shrill voice and tears met us as we reached the verandah.

Nell's always calm voice was audible between the sobs. 'It's okay. Look you're alive and anything lost can be replaced.'

The voice was even more shrill. 'But it is my passport. How can I get that replaced? I have no other ID.'

My eyes narrowed again as we walked inside; Rafe and Evie were close behind me as I held the two Ziplock bags out of sight behind my back.

I guess I wasn't feeling terribly sympathetic, and I tried to figure out why. I watched our mystery woman drop her head into her hands and sob some more. Maybe because it was my island, and I only wanted people I invited here for the moment. It would soon be overrun with guests when we opened the resort. I didn't want a stunning looking intruder changing the dynamics of our group.

Eliza's dark hair had dried, and some colour had come back into her cheeks. She was certainly the woman whose photo was in the passport behind my back.

'Pip?' Rafe's soft voice held surprise and he nudged me. I looked back at him and he gestured to the two bags.

Guilt flooded through me. I was being a suspicious bitch. The poor woman had almost drowned and I was being precious. After all, we could have been dealing with a body on the beach instead of a crying woman.

I walked over and crouched down beside the lounge where Nell was trying to soothe her.

'Eliza?' I said. 'It's okay. Evie found your kayak.'

She looked up and when she saw Rafe behind me, the colour leached from her face. Her eyes were wide as she stared up at him.

He smiled. 'Hello, I'm Rafe. I live across the bay.' As usual his words were cultured and polite, and his posh accent made me smile.

Eliza leaned back and an expression akin to relief crossed her face. 'You found it? You found my kayak?'

'Evie did.' It was about time I was a bit more welcoming. 'I'm Pippa, this is Evie, and you've met Rafe.'

'And we've already introduced ourselves.' Tam had been watching from the kitchen doorway.

'Where is my kayak now?' Eliza jumped to her feet. 'Is it damaged? Is it okay?'

'It's fine.' I held out the two bags. 'We wanted to check it was yours and we found these in the front well.'

Eliza's hand went to her chest and she closed her eyes. 'Thank God.'

For a minute I thought she was going to faint, and I reached out, but she leaned across and took the bags from me.

'Thank you. Thank you so much.' She glanced down at the envelope with the money and a tinge of colour stained her cheeks. 'I always keep my money and valuables and my passport with me. I've met a few undesirables while I've been backpacking around the islands.'

'Don't thank me. Evie was the one who found the kayak.'

'Thank you, Evie, and thank you all. I am a very lucky person to have been rescued here.' She glanced across at Evie. 'You didn't find my pack with my clothes in the back hatch?'

Evie shook her head. 'I didn't look there. It was getting dark and the wind was coming up, so I just hooked it up to the tender and brought it in.'

'Your kayak is down on the beach.'

She stood. 'I'll go and look now.'

Rafe stepped forward. 'I'll go. You stay here. Tell me exactly what I'm looking for.'

'Just a small pack jammed into the back well behind the seat. My tent is on top and my shoes should be underneath. I travel lightly.'

'Okay, be back in a tick,' he said.

I didn't like the way Eliza looked at him.

I moved away and nodded to Tam. 'Dinner ready to go?'

The conversation around the dinner table was interesting to say the least. If it hadn't been for all of us hearing what Eliza had said on the beach about going fishing and paddling to get firewood, I would probably have doubted what I'd heard.

Rafe had brought her bag up and she'd changed into a pair of khaki shorts and a black T-shirt. Nell had taken her to one of the spare rooms at the back that we'd been painting and preparing for staff when we hired.

'Do you have a phone to call your friends?' I asked as Tam served out the boiled rice. 'They must be worried.'

She shook her head. 'I don't, but they're not really my friends. Just other travellers who were on the island when I arrived there. I don't know if any of them have a phone.'

I stared at her. 'We'll take the boat over as soon as it's light and drop you back there.'

She shook her head. 'There's no need for that.'

'You said they'd be worried,' I said.

'No. In these groups people come and go. They won't worry.'

'I thought you said you'd caught fish and you were getting firewood.'

'Did I?' Her wide forehead scrunched up in a frown. 'I don't remember that I was going to do that.'

'That's what you said.' I glanced at Nell as her knee touched mine beneath the table and she shook her head slightly.

'Tell us about your travels,' Nell said with a smile. 'I think you are brave to be paddling around the islands in an ocean kayak.' She chuckled. 'Living on an island is as brave as I get.'

Eliza took the plate of curry and rice that Tam held out before she answered. 'You live on the island?'

Nell nodded. 'It's Pippa's island, and this is her house.'

Rafe cleared his throat. 'Ahem.'

'Oh, and Rafe owns half the island. Sorry, Rafe.' Nell flicked him an apologetic smile.

'A fabulous place to live. I love these islands. I've been thinking of settling here.'

'You're from Brisbane?' I asked.

Eliza nodded. 'Recently. I grew up in New Zealand. I've always loved the water. My dad was a fisherman and we lived close to the water just like this.'

'I thought I detected a Kiwi accent. My boss at the Gold Coast was from Auckland.'

'You haven't always lived here?'

'No, Tam and Nell and I have been here about eight weeks. Evie joined us a couple of weeks later. We're developing a resort.' I couldn't help the pride in my voice. Now that we knew a little bit more about her, I was relaxing.

'That must be exciting.'

Tam laughed. 'I don't know that exciting is the word I'd use this week. I wouldn't care if I never held a paint brush again.'

'But you must admit it was worth it. The place is looking great.' I took the plate that Tam held out. 'And I love you for your painting skills as much as your cooking.'

'It smells delicious, thank you.' Eliza reached for the jug and poured water into her glass. 'So, you're renovating the house as a guesthouse yourselves? What about you, Rafe? Where do you fit in?'

'I'm just a neighbour,' he said but he held my gaze. 'I was here first, but we have come to an arrangement.'

'We have.' I held his gaze steadily and a flutter of anticipation tugged low in my belly. An arrangement where the terms were yet to be defined, but I was very happy with the pace we were working at.

'Pippa's a slave driver, but we love her,' Evie said. 'Best boss ever. I've been doing the gardens and planning the walking tracks and helping out with the painting.'

I pulled a face at her. 'Remember, I'm a friend before I'm a boss. We're all in this together.'

'What about you, Nell?' Eliza's expression was full of interest, and having an outsider look so impressed, reminded me of how much we'd achieved in such a short time. I was really lucky to have such good friends who had as much determination as I did to make this project succeed.

'I keep Pip on the straight and narrow looking after the finances.' Nell was calm and quiet as always.

'And she paints too.' Tam laughed. 'We all paint except for Pippa. We banned her because she made such a mess.'

'Hey, be careful how you talk about the boss,' I joked.

'So, you really are doing it all yourselves?'

Eliza asked.

'As much as we can. We will hire when we need to. We had contractors over from the mainland yesterday to pour the slabs for the huts.'

'You girls are incredible.' Eliza looked around the table at each of us, and for the first time, I let go of the suspicion that I had held. 'And when you open for business, you'll need more staff?' Her voice held a hopeful note as she looked at me.

'And before.' I put my fork down and tipped my head to the side. 'Why do you ask?'

'I'd be interested in applying if you were hiring.'

'What's your background? Qualifications?'

'I don't have any formal qualifications, but I can turn my hand to most things. My father taught me everything I needed to know. As well as our fishing business, we had a market garden and a small vineyard on Waiheke Island. I can fix a motor, use a hammer, dig a garden, make wine, catch fish, and'—she was really beautiful when she smiled—'I wield a mean paintbrush.'

I nodded slowly. 'What are your plans? I mean, I—we—don't want someone who's not committed to our project. Someone who might up and leave if the going got tough.' I looked around the table. 'I trust these three girls with my life.'

'I have no plans,' she said simply.

'Let us think about it. We'll talk in the morning.'

Chapter 5

Marissa: Croatia

The first week on *Lady Calypso* was idyllic. It had taken Marissa a while to work up the courage to tell Rosco that she had no idea how to cook the fish he'd caught the second morning on board. The first night they'd sailed across to the island, they'd dined on the fresh crusty loaf and olives that Rosco had picked up at the marina where his boat was berthed when he wasn't on it.

Marissa had looked over at the heavily wooded shore. 'Is there a town? Or just that village you mentioned?' All she could see was hills covered with tall pine trees, and the occasional rocky outcrop. As she stared at the forest, she noticed there was a track through the trees.

'Only the village, but we won't leave the boat yet. I don't want to share my new wife.' Rosco pulled her close and nuzzled his lips into her neck.

'But where will we eat? And shop?

'I have enough provisions on board for you to cook. And I will catch more fish for us.'

'Cook?' Marissa shook her head slowly. 'I don't cook.'

Rosco pulled his head back and stared at her.

'Every woman cooks.'

'I beg your pardon?' Marissa took a step back.

'I said women cook. As my wife, you will cook my meals.'

Marissa folded her arms as her temper

pinged. 'I'm very sorry, Rosco. I don't agree with your attitude. It is a bit old fashioned. Perhaps we should have discussed this more.'

Instead of falling in lust, she thought.

'Oh, *cara mia,* already you give me grounds for divorce.' His mouth was set in a straight line. 'You cannot cook the fish that I caught for us?'

'Oh . . . oh . . .' Her mouth had dropped open and heat rushed to her face until she saw his dancing eyes. 'Oh, you are teasing me!'

'Come here.' His bare skin had pressed against hers—Marissa still couldn't get used to her husband wandering about the boat naked—most of the time she insisted on leaving her bikini on.

'There is no one here to see you,' he said, but she shook her head.

'I don't feel comfortable . . . yet.' It was taking her a while to adjust to being married and in one person's exclusive company, but she had no regrets. She just had to make some adjustments.

'I will take you down to the galley and I will teach you how to cook fish. It will be my pleasure.'

She closed her eyes and his lips pressed butterfly kisses along her jaw. 'There's only one thing I will insist on,' she murmured.

His lips paused on their journey to her mouth and his voice was stern. 'Insist on? You will never insist on anything.'

She opened her eyes and his dark eyes were intent on hers.

'Oh yes, I will,' she said. 'I insist that you put clothes on if we are working in the galley. I would hate to see'—her eyes dropped, and she summoned a sultry smile— 'any part of you damaged in the galley.'

He pulled her close again and his breath tickled her ear. 'As you are concerned about my safety, and your future pleasure, I will abide by your rule.' He lowered his voice. 'For this one time, you can tell me what to do.'

A niggle of uneasiness settled in her chest.

The next morning Marissa lay on their soft bed staring up at the open hatch in their cabin. Rosco was on the deck already, but she hadn't heard any noise apart from a splash and then his feet on the steps as he'd climbed onboard a few minutes later.

Maybe he was swimming off a hangover, she thought. She hoped so.

He deserved one after last night.

All was quiet now as the boat rocked gently in the slight breeze that blew down through the thickly forested slope.

Marissa rolled over and buried her face in the pillow. How many people had their first fight within five days of being married?

It had all started last night when they were sitting on the deck having a drink before dinner. She'd been nervous about preparing the fish—even with his help—and as the sun slipped behind the wooded forest Rosco turned to her.

'What are you going to prepare with the fish I will cook with you?'

'Um? With the fish?'

He shook his head slowly. 'Yes. A salad? Perhaps some *patatas*?'

'Ah . . . *patatas*?' Marissa said. 'I thought we were going to prepare the meal together.'

'This one time I will cook the fish up here. I think it's time for you to begin to prepare the rest of the meal. And to learn.' He drained his wine glass and refilled it, and his eyes narrowed before she looked away.

'Okay.' She put her wine glass on the table in front of the deck sofa that they were curled up on. As she stood Rosco ran his hand lightly down her leg. 'You are a very beautiful woman; Marissa I am very fortunate to have you as my wife.'

'And I you, my love.'

His dark eyes sent a delicious shiver down her spine and she felt like pinching herself. How could it be that two months ago she and Sienna had been planning their holiday to Italy, and now here she was, married to a gorgeous Italian and on a beautiful yacht on the Adriatic Sea. Marissa leaned down and brushed a kiss on Rosco's cheek.

'Let's see if you say that after you have your dinner,' she said with a laugh.

His brow wrinkled in a frown as he stared up at her. 'What do you mean?'

'You'll see,' she said.

Well, Rosco had seen, and he wasn't impressed, but she was less than impressed with his over-the-top reaction.

She done her best with what was in the galley. It was hard enough figuring out how to light the stupid gas thing to boil the potatoes—it was very different to what she had in her flat back in London—and then find a suitable saucepan, and figure out how to get water out of the complicated tap thing over the sink. Marissa was determined not to ask for help.

But when she had succeeded—and managed to throw together a salad and mash the potatoes—she took great care in arranging the food on the plates, before placing them on the dining table adjacent to the galley. She stood back and smiled as she put a sprig of some green stuff on the potatoes before she lit a candle.

'Rosco, dinner is ready,' she called up to the deck. A minute later he came down the stairs carrying a fry pan. His expression was hard to read as he lifted the fish fillets onto the plates next to the piles of mash.

He sat at the table and had not spoken as they dined on the simple meal. The salad could probably have done with some sort of dressing, but she hadn't been able to find anything in the cupboard. But it wasn't too bad; the fish was divine, and the rest was . . . well, it was edible.

And Marissa cleared her entire plate. After a while, the silence broken only by the clatter of cutlery on the fine china plates became uncomfortable. She put her fork on her plate and looked at Rosco. He was staring at his plate; he had eaten his fish, but the salad and mash was still there. She had to break this awful silence.

'Thank you for cooking the fish. It was delicious. What was that herb you sprinkled on it?'

He didn't answer. His expression was tight as he stood and pushed the plate away without a word. Marissa's stomach dropped when he turned his back without answering.

There was no way she was going to beg for attention or conversation.

Her husband disappeared up the stairs; his

bare feet making no sound on the smooth timber adding to the uncomfortable silence. She sipped her wine and sat there waiting for him to come back down. After fifteen minutes, an empty glass of wine and a stomach roiling with nerves, she stood and cleared the table, rinsed the dishes and went up to the deck. On the way she topped up her glass of wine for some Dutch courage.

Sod him. She would ignore him until he apologised for his childish behaviour.

Rosco was sitting on the front of the boat with his legs hanging over the side and as he turned, she got a whiff of sweet cigar smoke.

'I didn't know you smoked,' she said as she settled on the deck cushion to his left. He turned around and his face was cold.

'Did you need to know that? Would you have agreed to be my wife, if you had known?'

'Of course I would.'

Marissa would have liked to have said 'Perhaps not,' but his mood was too strange for her to be honest. The Rosco who was sitting next to her was not the kind gentle man she'd promised to love honour and—*oh, shit*—obey.

He drew in deeply and a moment later she held her breath as she was engulfed in a cloud of smoke.

Marissa hated smoking; watching her grandfather suffer for months before lung cancer had taken him had been one of the hardest times of her life. She had only been ten, and Gramps had insisted on spending his last days at Meynell Manor. When she was home from boarding school she had sat by his side and helped him with his crosswords. It had turned her off smoking—and crosswords—for life.

Rosco turned his back to her again and she put her glass on the deck and damn, never one for conflict, she couldn't help herself. She tentatively touched his shoulder. His skin was warm and damp beneath her fingers, but he shrugged away from her touch.

Marissa swallowed. 'Is there something wrong?' she said quietly.

'That English stodge that you put on my plate was *pasto disgustoso*,' he said.

'I don't know what your words mean, but I guess from your tone that it was unacceptable.' She tried to lighten the mood with a chuckle and then swallowed it back. 'Did you need to know that I couldn't cook before you asked me to marry you?' she asked parroting his words of a few moments ago.

Rosco reached for her and took her wrist between fingers that pressed tightly against her skin. 'I would assume that any woman who agreed to marry a man would be able to cook.'

Marissa's jaw dropped and she tipped her head to the side wondering if he was joking. How could a man say that—or even think that—in the twenty-first century?

She tried to brush it off as a joke. 'I warned you. I told you that you would think differently after dinner, Rosco darling. I was very spoiled to grow up in a home where we had a cook, and—'

'*Non mi stai ascoltando.*'

'What does that mean?'

'It means you are not listening to me. Well, you will learn.'

'I beg your pardon?'

'You will learn to cook. I will not be served food like you serve me before.' Rosco's accent thickened along with his temper, and he waved the cigar around. Marissa leaned back before it could touch her face.

She pulled her arm from his grip unable to believe that the man speaking to her was the same gentle man she spent the last few weeks with. In those weeks there had never been a cross word or an expression or tone like she was seeing and hearing now. His behaviour was unacceptable. She clenched her hands by her side as her temper began to boil.

Perhaps he has had too much to drink.

She glanced at the small tumbler that was next to him. Some sort of spirit over ice filled the glass.

Fine, if he wanted to sit up here by himself and sulk over some potato mash, he was welcome to his own company.

'I'm tired. I'm going to bed.' Marissa went to stand but he held her wrist. This time it hurt.

'You will go to bed when I am ready for you to leave me.'

She tried to pull her arm back, but Rosco was holding on too tightly for her to free her arm from his grip.

'Let go of me. Now.' Her teeth were clenched, and her words were terse as disbelief flooded through her.

He did as she requested, and his eyes glittered dangerously in the moonlight.

'You have obviously had too much to drink, Rosco. I will leave you to it. I am tired and I am going to bed. Now.' Her words were clipped as she turned and strode along the deck to the stairwell.

Mocking words followed her down to the cabin. 'Ah, the poor little rich girl is worn out from trying to cook a decent meal for her poor husband.' The sound of a bottle clinking against his glass followed Rosco's slurred words.

For a while she considered locking the cabin door and make him sleep on the deck, but with the mood he was in she was afraid of what he'd do.

Afraid? She bit her lip as she began to wonder who she had married.

Just before dawn as the sky lightened through the hatch above, she was aware of Rosco putting his arm around her waist. She squeezed her eyes shut and fell into a deep sleep.

When she opened them again, sunlight was streaming into the cabin, but she was alone.

Marissa closed her eyes again as she lay there. She couldn't believe or understand the change in Rosco. The first rosy flush of married life wasn't supposed to wear off for at least six months. She had heard her mother tell both of her sisters that when they had come home whining about their husbands.

She had been married six days and they had fought over bloody mashed potatoes. Thinking about her family sent a fresh surge of guilt through Marissa. She still hadn't contacted them. Maybe they weren't close anymore, and she was a grown woman with her own life but no matter how distant their relationship was they were still her parents and she should tell them she was married.

Every time she had gone to phone home, Rosco had distracted her. Climbing out of bed, she pulled a robe over her satin pyjamas and dug into her handbag for her phone. The screen stayed black when she held the power button in.

Damn, the battery was flat, and she didn't have a charger with her; she and Sienna had shared one as they'd travelled.

Marissa put the phone on the shelf beside the bed and frowned as she heard voices from above.

Who could it be?

When she had stormed off to bed last night, *Lady Calypso* had been the only boat in the bay.

Now there was a strange voice coming from above as Rosco spoke to someone. Slipping out of her PJs and robe, she headed for the tiny bathroom. Once she was dressed in her bikini and sarong and had pulled her hair up with a clip, she made her way up to the top deck wondering what sort of reception she was going to get, and angry with herself that she had let Rosco speak to her like that.

And angry that she was worried about it.

'Is Celeste still asleep?' The unfamiliar voice reached her as she stood at the doorway. Rosco's back was to her and all she heard was a chuckle and a murmured reply that was too quiet to hear.

Celeste? Who the hell was Celeste?

She stepped out on to the deck and glanced across to the bay. A long white sloop that had obviously seen better days was moored quite close to them. Her gaze moved back to the deck where an olive-skinned man with dark hair stood facing her. His gaze fixed on her and she tightened the knot of her sarong more firmly as his eyes raked her from head to toe.

His smile was lazy as he nodded to Rosco and her husband turned to her with a wide smile.

Relief filled her as he opened his arms wide.

'My darling, you are finally awake. Come and meet my good friend.'

She walked slowly across the deck to join them and leaned into Rosco as his hands held her waist.

Gently.

She looked up at him, and an unspoken apology crossed his expression before he leaned down and brushed his lips across hers. He whispered against her lips. 'I'm sorry. So very sorry.'

She pressed her mouth against his briefly in acknowledgement, but her smile was tight when she pulled back. It was going to take more than a whispered apology to appease her. Rosco's arm went around her shoulder.

'Marissa, this is my dear sailing friend, Ren. Ren, this is my lovely wife. Marissa has brought my dreams to life. We are on our honeymoon.'

Ren's glance was inscrutable as he reached over and took her hand. As he bent over, she noticed his hair was tied back with a leather tie. He brushed his lips across her fingers. *'Enchanté'*

Heat filled her face as he continued to hold her hand. Finally, he let go but his eyes stayed on her.

'It is a pleasure to meet you too, Ren.' She gestured to the sloop and for the first time saw that two other boats were anchored on the other side of the bay. Their idyllic private location had gotten busy overnight. 'Which is your boat?'

'Which do you think would be mine?' His voice held a delightful French lilt that sent a shiver down her spine.

Gawd, what on earth am I thinking? She'd always been a sucker for a French accent, but she was a married woman now, and it wasn't right to let another man's sexy voice give her the shivers.

Although he *was* a very good-looking man. He was a lot fitter and more muscled than Rosco, and when she looked closely, it was clear he was closer to her age than her husband's. Her glance swivelled to the three boats, and then back to him.

'The first one,' she said. '*Sea Dreaming.*'

'Not only beautiful, but very clever too, Rosco. You speak French?'

This time she didn't shiver, as she sensed a slightly patronising tone in his words. 'A little. Only schoolgirl French.' She wasn't sure she liked him.

'Marissa and I were considering going out for dinner in the village tonight.' Rosco said. 'We would be delighted if you would join us.'

Marisa raised her eyebrows and stared, but Rosco ignored her.

We were? Unless she'd been asleep when he'd mentioned it, he was telling porkies.

What happened to 'I don't want to share my new wife with anyone'?

Ren demurred. 'Thank you, but I watch my euros when I am at sea.'

'I insist. You will be my guest. I must owe you ten dinners by now, my friend.'

Marissa didn't miss the significant look that they exchanged. 'I'm going for a swim,' she said. 'It was good to meet you, Ren. Perhaps I will see you at dinner. It would be a pleasure to have you join us.'

'If you are sure?'

She nodded. 'Of course.'

In one lithe movement Ren was over the deck and into the small rowboat that was tied up on the side of *Lady Calypso.*

Rosco looped his arm around her shoulder as they stood and watched the small boat as he rowed across the water.

Marissa was determined not to be the one to break the silence. She was still feeling fragile and hurt from last night. She stood still as Ren pulled up next to the sloop and climbed on board.

Rosco's breath warmed her cheek and he moved his hands ever so gently on the bare skin above her sarong. She relaxed as his lips settled in the curve of her neck. 'Forgive me?'

Her vision blurred as her eyes filled with tears and hovered on her lashes, threatening to fall. She bit her lip, still not wanting to speak.

'It was the *Sljiovica,* the plum brandy. It always makes me angry. I am so, so sorry.' His voice was deep and shook a little.

Her hands crept up around his neck and she rested her head on his shoulder. 'You frightened me.'

'Never again, I promise. I am so sorry, my darling girl.'

Chapter 6

Pippa: Pentecost Island

Rafe left after we had eaten Tam's amazing white chocolate and ginger cheesecake. I offered to walk him as far as the beach and Eliza's gaze settled on us as we stood at the door together and he said goodnight to everyone.

'Thank you for dinner, Tam,' he said politely. 'Night, Nell, goodnight Evie.' He turned to Eliza. 'It was a pleasure to meet you, Eliza and I'm pleased that if you had to be rescued it was on our island.'

He was such a nice guy—an absolute gentleman—and as much as I tried not to I couldn't help comparing him with Darren and the other guys I thought I'd fallen for in my past.

Rafe was different and the feelings I held for him already frightened me. What if he decided he didn't like me anymore? I honestly think it would have been enough to have me scurrying for the mainland. The resort and Aunty Vi's house were running a bit of a second now to how I felt about him. That night I had first seen him at Hamilton Island had been a life changer, although it had taken a rescue from a tree for me to realise how quickly I had fallen for him.

We were both quiet as we left the house and walked along the path to the beach. The wind had dropped, and the clouds had cleared; the rising moon promised a spectacular night as soon as it cleared the hill to the east. I let out a soft sigh. This island was one of the most beautiful places on earth. Happiness trickled through me and I embraced it; it wasn't a feeling I was terribly familiar with, but one that seemed to be overtaking me more and more since I had come to my island.

Rafe held my hand and I let my fingers lace through his. They were warm and held mine gently; it was typical of the man he was—gentle and patient—and that sort of guy was totally out of the realm of my experience.

I looked down at the ground as we strolled along.

Why me? Why had he picked me? I'd never had much self-confidence, and I knew I had to work to get over it, and to trust my feelings, and to trust Rafe.

We reached the beach just as the moon cleared the hill. A shaft of golden moonlight lit up the bay and the slight ripples on the water headed out into the passage in a circular pattern. The soft whoosh of the small waves pushing onto the beach was the only sound.

It was so beautiful I held my breath as we stood and watched the moonlight spread across the bay.

Two hands touched my shoulders and pulled me back gently. The way Rafe put his arms around me and tucked me back against his chest was like every move he made—slow and considered.

His lips ran slowly down my cheek and lingered at the edge of my mouth until I turned to meet him.

We stood bathed in moonlight as our lips met, and goose bumps ran down my neck and arms. No other man had ever made me feel like this. It wasn't the sexual attraction—although that was there in bucketloads—it was knowing that Rafe cared about me. About Pippa Carmichael the person.

As damaged as I was.

Our breathing quickened as his lips and tongue explored mine, and I responded.

I was lost as his hands lowered to hold me closer and I was left in no doubt about the strength of his desire.

'Will you come home with me tonight, Pip?'

As much as I was tempted, I shook my head.

'When?' he said softly. 'I don't know I can wait much longer. I dream about you in my bed every night.'

'Soon,' I whispered. I wasn't brave enough to tell him that I was scared if we slept together it would all come to an end. Like most good things in my life always had.

'You're hesitant, aren't you?' he said voicing the thoughts I had never told him. He was getting to know me very well.

'A little,' I admitted. 'I would like to come home with you'—I lifted my head and held his dark gaze— 'and I will soon, but tonight isn't the right time. Not with our mermaid spending the night over at my house. It wouldn't be the right thing to do. Leaving her there with the other girls, I mean.'

Rafe rested his forehead against mine. 'You are a good person, Pippa.'

'I'm not really.' I relaxed into his hold. 'But it's okay if you think that.'

'Oh, I do and a lot more than that. You know that we are going to be together, don't you? There will only be one problem that I can see.'

I moved back a little with a frown. 'A problem?'

'When the time comes would you be happy to leave your place and move into mine? I know how special it is to you and I—'

'Whoa. You're moving too fast. There's a lot you need to know about me before we think about that.' I put my fingers to his lips. 'It's only a house, Rafe. But if it does ever come to that, I can't see there will be a problem. You have a very suitable house.' I smiled.

'It's not your opinion of the house that matters to me.'

'I know. I was teasing. I think you are a very suitable man too.'

'That's what I was hoping for.' His arms tightened around me and I felt cocooned, and safe as his lips rested against mine.

'I was hoping we could spend tonight together as I have to go away.' His words vibrated against my mouth. I stiffened in his hold and moved back from him as my newfound serenity fled.

'Away? Where to?'

Not that it was my business.

'Come back here.' He pulled me close again. 'You have to trust me, Pip. I have to go back to London. Just for a short visit.'

Rafe had told me all about his divorce, but now my doubts crept back in.

'I have to see Bryant—my publisher.'

Sweet relief filled me. It was nothing to do with his ex.

'Because it's been a while between books, and because I'm not prepared to do a world tour, he wants me to do a digital marketing campaign. I have to go over there and record some interviews and some promo clips for the new book. I tried to talk him into doing over Skype, but he said the quality wasn't good enough. He's accepted that I won't do a personal tour, so I gave in on the digital stuff, even though it means a long flight over and back.'

'I'll miss you,' I said.

He held my gaze. 'I'd love you to come with me, but I didn't ask you because I know that you are so close to opening and you've got a lot of work ahead.'

'Once we get up and running, I'll go anywhere with you, Rafe.'

'That makes me one very happy man. I won't be gone long this time, and I want to be back here for your opening. I wouldn't miss that for the world. In fact, I told Bryant unless he could get this stuff organised in the next two weeks, I wouldn't come.'

'It's not far off.' Thinking about the resort put Eliza back into my thoughts. 'Come and sit for a while. I want to get your take on our mermaid.'

We settled on a wide fallen log that had come down in the recent cyclone.

'She was a very lucky woman that you were on the beach this afternoon,' Rafe said as he put his arm around my shoulders, and I leaned back against him

'She was.' I nodded slowly.

'What are you worried about?' he asked.

'I don't know. I've just got a sense that she's not telling us everything. She changed her story about the fishing and the firewood when she was pressed. And all that money and that ring seems a bit suss.'

'Does she have to tell us all about herself?'

I stared out over the water. 'She was more than happy to give us all the details of her childhood in New Zealand.'

'She doesn't know any of us. And she doesn't know us well enough to trust us.' He nudged me with his shoulder. 'And look who's talking, anyway.'

'True.'

'She said she could turn her hand to most things. Why don't you give her a trial run? You were going to advertise anyway, weren't you?'

I nodded. 'I was.'

'And forgive me if I'm overstepping the mark here, but I'm getting the impression that this is a business that seems to be hiring women?'

'I guess it is. It wasn't intentional, but it's turned out that way. 'I turned around and grinned at him. 'Why? Did you want a job?'

His chuckle was deep. 'The only thing I want at the moment is being denied to me. But I can wait. I hear the boss at Ma Carmichael's is one tough lady.'

'I'm determined to make this work, Rafe. It means so much that Aunty Vi left it to me.'

'And I have no doubt that you will. I'm looking forward to seeing it up and running and you having some free time.'

'Okay. It's time I headed back.' His rough whiskers grazed my fingers as I reached up and took his face between my hands. 'Thank you for being patient with me.'

'Sweetheart, I will wait as long as it takes.'

'Just don't go meeting anyone else in London and deciding to stay there.'

'There's no chance of that.'

The moon disappeared as he lowered his head to mine.

Chapter 7

Marissa

Ren picked us up in his boat and he rowed us around the southern point of the secluded bay where we were now anchored with several other boats. Three more boats had come in since the morning, and there had been many hand waves and greetings called out as they motored past us.

Rosco hadn't seemed to mind the end of our isolation, and our private honeymoon. We had spent most of the day sunbathing on the deck and jumping into the crystal-clear water when we needed to cool down. He had been very affectionate all day and we had gone down to the cabin for a rest after lunch, and he had proceeded to show me how sorry he was.

My confidence had been damaged by his drunken behaviour and although I assured him—several times—that all was forgiven, a part of me stayed wary.

I didn't mention anything about cooking or learning to cook in case his bad temper resurfaced. I dressed in a brightly coloured dress—one I had bought on the Isle of Capri at the beginning of the holiday with Sienna. As I dressed, I remembered the flat battery phone in my phone.

'Rosco,' I called up the stairs. 'Do you have a phone charger that will suit my phone. My battery is flat, and I must call my family.

'No point here, *cara*. There is no service,' he called from the deck.

'Oh, okay.' I put my phone back on the

cupboard, but a niggle of worry stayed with me. Even Sienna didn't know where I was. When we'd said goodbye to her in Florence, I'd thought I was heading for the airport and France.

This was a very big step I'd taken. Away from all that was familiar and away from my family and friends.

As we rowed into the next bay, Rosco and Ren chatted in the front of the boat. I leaned back trailing my hand in the warm water, lost in my thoughts. If it hadn't been for that incident last night, I would have been in a world of happiness, but Rosco's ugly behaviour had taken away from the beauty around us.

We soon entered the small bay through a narrow entrance that was surrounded by steep rocky hills. I thought Rosco had said it was a long walk to the village. Along the foreshore were some old buildings where fishing boats were moored at a stone wharf. It was warm, protected from the wind and the water was so clear I could see the sandy bottom.

Ren tied the boat to the end of the wharf and stood next to Rosco and they both held out a hand to help me up from the rowboat. As we walked along the stone wall leading to a couple of *tavernas* fronting the small harbour, a cheery voice called out from one of the doorways ahead.

'Rosco!'

My husband hurried along the wall and spoke to the burly man who had hailed him for a couple of minutes before Ren and I caught up to him.

'You are happy to be married, Marissa?' Ren's voice was quiet, and I thought what a strange question to ask a woman on her honeymoon.

'I am,' I said firmly and hurried over to where Rosco was waiting.

'Mauro,' Rosco said as he held his hand out to me. 'This is my beautiful wife, Marissa.'

The older man took my hand and pumped it in a tight handshake. 'Ah, a beautiful wife. What an occasion. Come to my *taverna* and we will celebrate. My brother will bring out the new *Sljiovica*. We shall toast your marriage and wish you many children.'

Sljiovica! I certainly hoped not.

Rosco looked sheepish and caught my eye and sent me a reassuring smile. 'I think we will begin with a beer and then have some of that excellent wine from your vineyard, Mauro,' he said. 'The dozen bottles I took back to Florence after our last visit were very popular with my friends.'

Mauro ushered us inside and I was seated between Ren and Rosco. Ren's behaviour seemed distant now, but I didn't care. I was going to enjoy this experience.

Mauro brought a procession of relatives from the back of the taverna, and we met his mother who was the cook, as well as being the local cheesemaker and baker. His grandmother—an elderly woman with several teeth missing and dressed in a black dress—apparently looked after the gardens that supplied the produce. She hurried back outside after a brief greeting, and then we met Mauro's son who supplied the fish to the kitchen.

Once the introductions had been made, Mauro placed three carafes on the table: red wine, white wine and water.

'*Gemist* or *bevanda?*' he asked me as he

picked up the glass that was in front of my setting.

I looked to Rosco for help, but he was chatting.

Ren leaned forward. 'Do you prefer to drink white or red wine, Marissa?' He glanced up at Mauro and lowered his voice. 'What the Croatians do to perfectly good wine is sacrilege to a Frenchman. The two words mean white wine with water, or red wine with water.'

'Which is white?' I asked.

'*Gemist*,' he replied.

I turned to Mauro. 'Then I will have *gemist*, please.'

Mauro nodded and hurried away and when he returned, he opened a bottle of sparkling water and added some to my glass before topping it up with white wine.

Rosco gestured to my glass. 'Forget the beer, my friend, I will have the white as well.'

There were no menus to choose from, but we dined on freshly caught scarfish and anchovies. By the end of the meal not only was I an expert on the varieties of fish, his mother had also given me the recipe for the baked fish meal we had eaten.

As she listed the ingredients in halting English, Rosco caught my eye and nodded with a wide smile.

I guess that was considered to be my first cooking lesson.

It was very late when we headed back to the wharf, with Mauro eliciting a promise from Rosco that we would return tomorrow night. It had been a pleasant evening, marred only for me when I heard Mauro mention the name Celeste to Ren when his mother was talking to me. I had strained to hear the conversation, but they had moved away. Rosco rowed the boat back as he had drunk very little with the meal and I had been pleased when he had declined the plum brandy.

We said goodnight to Ren, and Rosco waited until he got back to his boat safely, before he came down to join me in the cabin.

He nuzzled his lips into my neck and cupped my breast with a gentle hand. 'Did you enjoy your evening, my dear?'

I nodded as I leaned against him. He ran his fingers through my hair; I had just removed the clip that had held my blonde hair away from my face.

My confidence had returned, and I looked up at him as his lips descended towards mine. 'Rosco? Who is Celeste?'

He stopped and stared at me. 'Who has been talking to you of Celeste?'

'No one spoke to me, but I have heard her name mentioned a few times.'

His fingers tightened in my hair and I flinched as my hair was pulled.

'Ouch. That hurt.'

'I'm sorry. My ring caught on your hair.' His voice was hard.

My eyes stung with tears as my head throbbed where he had tugged at my hair.

'So who is Celeste?' I persisted when Rosco removed his hand. He still held my arm with his other hand, and I looked down. I actually had a bruise where he had held me too tightly last night, but I hadn't worried as my skin was so fair, I bruised easily.

'She is dead. She is a woman that Ren used

to travel with.'

'Oh. I'm sorry to hear of his tragedy.'

'Yes, it was very sad, so please don't mention her name in front of him.

He was lying. I had heard Ren's words yesterday.

I lay beside Rosco that night, until I heard his breathing change telling me he was asleep, and then I crept quietly out of the cabin and went and sat on the deck looking at the stars until I became sleepy.

In the end I didn't have to watch what I said around Ren, as his boat was gone the next morning. Rosco was extremely attentive over breakfast, and I was pleased when he discussed our plans with me.

'We will sail back to Dubrovnik in three days and then we will fly straight to London. Is that suitable to you?'

I nodded, very relieved to hear that our sojourn on this tiny boat would not be for much longer. If I was truthful with myself, I was finding it boring, even though it was supposed to be our honeymoon.

'As soon as we are in phone service again, I'll charge my phone and call my parents to let them know we are coming.'

'Shall we just surprise them? That would be more fun,' he said.

I shook my head. 'You don't know my parents. A surprise visit would send my mother into a spin.'

'A spin? I do not know what that means.'

'It means she will like to get organised. Super organised. She'll pull out all stops and you'll have to endure a six-course meal in the formal dining room, she'll invite her friends who she considers to be landed gentry, and we'll be put on show.'

'I do not like the sound of that visit. What do you feel about it?' he asked.

'I will hate every minute of it.'

His hands linked behind my back. 'Perhaps I have a better idea.'

Chapter 8

Pippa: Pentecost Island

Rafe flew to Brisbane out of Hamilton Island airport on the first leg of his trip to London, a week after Eliza arrived. It had been an interesting week; he'd been busy finalising his book, and I'd not spent a lot of time with him. I'd put Eliza on the payroll; her skills, and her work ethic had blown me away. She took on every small job I gave her with enthusiasm, finished it quickly and cleaned up after she'd finished.

In fact, I'd been pleasantly surprised when I'd gone into the tool shed a couple of days ago; it was organised and tidy and Eliza had used the labelling thing I'd bought—and never used—to give each tool a home. She seemed to have recovered from her mishap; she didn't talk about it—it was as though she wanted to forget about her near drowning. The other girls must have picked up on that as her arrival on our island hadn't been mentioned again. Her kayak was now underneath the house and she'd settled into a room at the back. Out of the four spare bedrooms she'd opted for the smallest.

Rafe must have been reading my thoughts as we sat together in the departure lounge. 'How's the work progressed this week?'

I know I looked smug. 'Would you believe we're ahead of schedule? We should be ready to open the bar to day visitors when you come back.'

'Maybe I should stay away from you more often? Like I have this week?' He put on a sad face.

'No, it's not you distracting me when you come over; it's Eliza being there. She's been a huge help.'

'It's turned out okay then?'

'It has. She's got a very logical mind. With her help, we got the frame of the first hut up in a couple of hours.' I chuckled. 'Tam and I were trying to read the instructions, but Eliza and Nell had the timber sorted while we arguing about where to start.' I reached over and slipped my arm through his; I found it hard not to touch Rafe when we were together. His fingers closed over mine and I smiled.

'You won't do anything silly over there, will you?' It was the most diplomatic way I could ask him what he would be doing without being too intrusive.

His fingers caressed mine. 'What silly things do you think I could get up to?'

'Um, you might decide you like the cool climate again?' Spring had hit with a vengeance and the humidity on Pentecost Island had skyrocketed.

He dropped a kiss on the top of my head. 'What about you? You might decide the heat is too much for you here while I'm gone. You might leave.'

I shook my head. 'No chance of that.'

'Ditto,' he said with a grin and my heart gave a little flip.

'I'm really going to miss you, you know,' I said playing with his fingers.

'You'll keep busy, you have good friends to keep you company and I'll be back before you know it. But you know what, Pippa? You have no idea how happy it makes me to know you'll miss me.'

I held his gaze and spoke softly. 'I can't imagine you not being there. You've been here since we landed on your island and disturbed your peace and quiet.'

'The best day of my life . . . so far,' he said as he leaned forward and brushed a kiss across my lips.

Rafe's flight was called, and when we stood up, he pulled me close. 'You be careful while I'm gone. Don't go climbing any trees or rescuing any mermaids.' His smile set my heart beating faster.

'You keep safe and hurry back to me,' I said.

'I will.' One last kiss, and he was out through the gate heading for the jet that would take him to Brisbane to pick up his international flight. He turned at the bottom of the steps and waved before he headed up into the jet.

I stood there in a daydream until the plane had taken off over the Coral Sea and then I made my way back to the marina, where Evie was waiting.

As much as Eliza was working out, I was still curious about her story, so Evie and I had planned to go to Lindeman and Little Lindeman Islands on the way back to our island, just to make sure no one was looking for her. I'd asked Jiminy, my school friend on Hamilton Island, if he'd heard anything about a missing kayaker when I'd seen him at the marina, but he'd heard nothing, and if there was anything to hear, Jiminy would know; he always had his ear to the ground.

'Done all Tam's shopping?' I called to Evie as I hurried towards her boat. I was pleased to see her waiting for me; the marina was adjacent to the airport, so it hadn't taken me long to get back.

'Yep, and I've stowed it below decks already. It took a bit of searching to find those Moroccan spices she was after, but I got them.'

'Great. You want a hand to cast off?'

She nodded and I untied the ropes and jumped aboard her small yacht. As we motored out of the marina, we passed a large white sloop.

'Hasn't she got beautiful lines?' Evie commented as the guy standing at the front waved to her.

I laughed. 'Who? The boat or did you mean to say he? He's seriously cute.'

'Ha ha. I meant the boat, even though she's had a long life, she is still a beautiful boat. Although he *was* a nice guy. A French dude. I gave him one of the flyers that Nell made up for our bar opening, and he said he might call into Pentecost on his way south.'

'And you're really hoping he does.'

Evie shrugged. 'A bit old for my tastes. Heading for forty, I'd say. His name's Phillipe, but he did have an accent to die for.'

'An old salt.' I checked out the boat as we pulled away. 'Looks like his boat's done some time at sea.'

'Yeah, he's travelling around the world. Said he's done the Mediterranean, the Adriatic, and has come down through Indonesia. Plans on spending some time in the Whitsundays. I told him to keep an eye out for our opening.'

'Maybe we'll see him out at the island. I can't believe how close the bar opening is.'

'Will Rafe be back in time?' Evie shot me a curious glance.

'Should be.'

'Which reminds me,' Evie said. 'How are you going to get the word out to the sailing community about the bar being open?'

I grinned. 'My speciality. I've put together a marketing campaign and it's almost ready to send out. I'm just waiting for Tam to finalise the menu for the bar food, and then we'll set a date.'

After the slabs had been poured for the huts, the concreters had come back and done the floor for the outdoor bar. The roof was up, and the outdoor furniture was stored at the back of the house. We were going to build a small shed at the side of the area to store the furniture in bad weather. I was looking at brochures to order a bar to go along the back wall, and the suppliers had assured me it would be ready in two weeks once I placed the order.

I was pretty proud of what we'd achieved in such a short time, and the Whitsunday tourism staff had said that there was a lot of local interest in our project.

I just hoped we hadn't made it too big to start with, and that we wouldn't fail.

'Stop chewing your fingernails, Pip. It will be fine. You are such a worrier.' Evie turned the boat out of the channel.

I removed my hand from my mouth. The three girls all knew me so well. 'I know. Can't help it. Are you still right to call into Lindeman?'

Evie nodded. 'Sure. You won't relax until you find out more about Eliza, will you?'

'I just want to check that no-one's worried about her. She doesn't seem to be.'

Evie regarded me for a long time before she

spoke. 'So why are you?'

I shrugged. 'Aunty Vi taught me to always trust my "spidey" sense and every time I think about how Eliza arrived it kicks in.'

Evie shook her head and increased the speed of the boat and we passed Catseye Beach on the northern side of the island. Her long dark hair flew wildly as we headed out into open water.

'If Eliza's not worried, why should we be? She's fitted in really well with us all so far.'

'Just humour me, Evie. Once I satisfy myself that there's no one looking for her, I'll let it go.'

We had no luck at Lindeman Island. The resort had closed about eight years ago, and I'd heard it had been sold to a Chinese consortium, but no development had taken place yet. It was sad to motor past and see the buildings standing faded and forlorn, with broken windows facing the sea. The pool was empty, and a couple of pool lounges were jammed up against the building. Plastic chairs littered the shore and I could even see a mattress lying in the long grass near the beach. I guess the last cyclone had finished off the resort. There were no kayaks or boats pulled up in the bay, so it looked like there was no-one on the island.

Evie swung the boat around, and we headed for Little Lindeman Island which was only a short distance from Pentecost. There were a few small islands to the west and the east, but Eliza had specifically said it was Little Lindeman where she'd been camping. It was a part of the national park, and there were sandy beaches on two sides of the island.

'There.' Evie pointed to the northern end of the wide expanse of sand. 'Look, there's a few kayaks like the one Eliza was in pulled up almost into the bush.'

'Let's go and have a chat.'

Evie set the anchor and we both climbed into the tender and headed for the shore. A man and a woman walked down to the water and helped pull us past the coral heads once the water was shallow.

'Hi there.' The guy had an American accent and his smile was wide. 'You looking to camp here tonight?"

I shook my head. 'No. We're just after some information.'

He looked at the woman and she frowned. 'What sort of information?'

'We wondered if you were missing any of your group?' Evie said pointing to the half a dozen kayaks lined up along the shore.

'Why?'

'We heard that a kayaker had gone missing from one of the islands and we thought we'd keep an eye out on our way home.' I crossed my fingers behind my back.

They both shook their heads.

'We haven't heard anything, but we only arrived here a couple of days ago,' the guy said. He pointed to the kayaks at the other end of the beach. That group has been here for a while, you could ask Johnny.'

I held out my hand. 'I'm Pippa, and this is Evie. We're over on Pentecost Island.'

The guy took my hand and shook it vigorously. They were a fit-looking couple in their fifties or so. 'I'm Jim and this is Margie. We've been kayaking around these beautiful Aussie islands for a few weeks now.'

Margie shook my hand and then Evie's. 'Pentecost Island? You live there? It's a magnificent geological formation. We plan on visiting in a week or two. After this weather passes.' She gestured to the clouds that were moving quickly up high. 'Some wind on the way, so we'll bunker in here until it calms again. I hope no one has gone missing.'

I grinned at Evie. 'If you do head our way, our bar and food will be up and running in a couple of weeks, I hope. We have a top chef on staff and you're more than welcome to camp over at Back Bay.'

'Sounds like a plan.' Jim nodded. 'Look, there's Johnny now.'

'Thanks. We'll head over and ask. Good to meet you both. I hope we see you over at our eco-resort. It's called Ma Carmichaels.'

'We'll call in for sure. Good to meet you gals,' Jim said.

We walked along the beach to where a young guy was pulling a kayak down towards the water.

'Johnny?' I called out.

He turned and waved. 'That's me. Hi there.'

Evie murmured quietly. 'Not bad. Not bad at all.'

I nudged her. 'You are a shocker.'

Although she was right, he was tanned and muscular.

'Hi, I'm Pippa and this is Evie.'

He waved again, less formal than the older American Jim. 'Come to stay for a while?' He smiled at Evie and I rolled my eyes.

'No, were looking for someone we know who we thought might have called in here.' I changed my story slightly.

'Yeah, there's been a few of us come and go here. Who're you looking for?'

'Eliza. A friend of ours from Brisbane.'

He stared at me for a moment and then shook his head. 'Sorry. No Eliza here since we arrived. There's been a few kayakers come and go, but we've met them all.'

'How long have you been here?'

'We've been here a couple of weeks.' He frowned. 'Actually, no. It's closer to three weeks. It's a great place to snorkel and the campsite back in the scrub's a beauty.'

'What about guys called Dylan and Alex? I think he was a friend she was travelling with.'

He rubbed his chin and nodded. 'Yeah, a guy called Dylan stayed here for a few nights. He left about ten days ago.'

Jackpot. It was ten days since Eliza had arrived on our island.

'And Eliza wasn't with him?' I persisted.

He shook his head. 'No. He was by himself. He wasn't kayaking; he moored his catamaran in the bay.'

'Okay, thanks. Looks like we've missed her. Thanks for the info,' I said. 'If you head back our way'—I pointed north— 'we've got a small resort opening up over on Pentecost Island. Call in and have a drink if you come our way.'

'Sounds like a plan. We'll be heading back to Hamo in a few days.'

I didn't care if we were open or not. I'd give them a drink. I was more interested to present Eliza with the group from Little Lindeman Island who apparently didn't know her from a bar of soap.

Chapter 9

Marissa: Croatia

The second week of our marriage passed without incident, and I began to enjoy myself again.

Well, apart from one incident.

I woke early one morning to hear Rosco's voice and I sat up in bed and poked my head through the hatch. He was on the forward deck and my eyes narrowed as I saw his phone pressed to his ear.

His back was to me, so I couldn't hear what he was saying, and he couldn't see me. I stared as he continued to talk, his gestures signalling his displeasure with something or someone. I was learning very quickly that things had to go the way my husband wanted, or he got in a mood.

Before he turned, I lowered myself back down and stretched out on the bed. Rosco had told me there was no phone service and I hadn't been able to call home. Although in one way it didn't matter now as he had talked me into surprising my parents with our visit. Perhaps his phone was on a local service, but it still surprised me that he hadn't offered it to me to use.

By the time he came back down to our cabin, I had dozed back off. I decided to keep the peace and not mention the phone. It didn't really matter. Once we got back to Italy, I'd buy a charger and some more credit for my phone. I was keen to talk to Sienna, as she was due to leave Italy late next week. I was also due back home so I would have to talk to my parents or turn up there by then.

A week later I was relieved when we left the boat and headed to the airport. My relief made me feel guilty because it was our honeymoon, but I put it down to being out of my comfort zone.

We landed in Florence, and when Rosco slipped into the gents I headed for the newsagent and found myself a phone charger.

Just that simple purchase brought my confidence back. I slipped it safely into my handbag.

Rosco smiled at me and held out his hand as we headed for the baggage carousel. I knew I looked good. We'd spent a lot of time sunbathing, and my skin was tanned, and my hair even blonder than usual. I'd managed to do the roots at the tiny sink in the boat when he was intent on his fishing one afternoon. I took his hand and squeezed it; it was good to be back where we'd met and married.

Rosco put his arm around me as we waited for a taxi. 'I can't wait to show you my villa,' he whispered.

'And I can't wait to see it,' I said.

The trip from the airport out into the countryside took an hour, and I widened my eyes when I saw the amount of money that my husband slipped the taxi driver after he had unpacked the suitcases. Rosco had ordered new luggage and new clothes for me, and they had been delivered to the hotel in Dubrovnik before we caught our flight. For a moment I felt strange, almost wishing I had my old backpack filled with familiar things.

An attractive woman—about my age—dressed in black and white opened the door and greeted us in English.

'Welcome home,' she said. The smile she gave to Rosco was wide, but it disappeared when she turned to me and nodded. '*Signora.*'

'Davina, this is my wife. Marissa, Davina will help you with anything that you need,' he said.

I wondered if she could cook.

'Hello, it is good to meet you.' I held out my hand, but she merely gave me another nod and turned away to Rosco.

'Lucia will have your meal ready at eight. She has gone down to the village to get some fresh herbs.'

Relief was sweet. Whoever Lucia was, she was obviously cooking, and I didn't have to worry.

I followed Rosco up a wide marble staircase trying not to show how impressed I was with the villa. He flung open the door to a large room with French doors that opened onto a small balcony overlooking the winding driveway that we had driven up.

The late afternoon sunbathed the tall pencil pines in a golden glow, and the pink brick of the outbuildings below us deepened in the fading light.

'It's breathtaking,' I said staring out over the vista, trying to accept that this was now my home. A peculiar feeling ran up my back and I shivered.

'Are you cold?' he said putting his arms around me. 'It is very different to being on my boat, isn't it?'

I smiled and nodded. 'It is, but it is very beautiful.'

'So are you, my darling. You are going to make my villa complete. I have been waiting a long time to find the right woman. You are perfect. Your blonde hair, your olive skin, your eyes'—his gaze ran down my body, and it felt as though I was being inspected rather than loved— 'you are exactly what I wanted.'

I suppressed the shiver this time. His words were strange and made me uncomfortable. It was as though I was a possession, not a wife.

Rosco dropped a kiss on my cheek. 'I have some work to do. I will call you when it is time to come down for dinner. I would like you to dress up please.'

I nodded slowly. 'I'll unpack. Will I get my bags from the foyer?''

'No, Willem will bring them up. I will ask him to get them now.'

'Willem? Just how many staff do you have?'

'Enough for my—our—needs,' he said with a brisk nod. 'I will see you at dinner.'

As promised, Willem—a young man who looked as though he was still in his teens—tapped on the door shortly after Rosco went downstairs.

He barely looked at me as I opened the door and he carried in the suitcases and placed them beside the wardrobe that lined the wall adjacent to the double window. He left without a word.

I glanced down at the bags and picking up my handbag I opened the French door and stepped out onto the balcony. A small wrought iron table and two chairs sat in the corner, touched by the last fingers of sunlight.

I dug in my bag for my phone. As soon as it was charged, I was going to call Sienna to see if we could catch up before she flew home. The compartment where I usually put it was empty and I dug deeper into the bag as I searched for it.

But my fingers came out empty each time. I upended the bag onto the table and frowned as the usual assortment that always filled my bag spilled on to the table, but there was no phone. I closed my eyes as I concentrated trying to remember where I had last seen it.

When I had discovered the battery was flat when we were on the boat, I'd put my phone on the cupboard in the cabin. I couldn't recall if I moved it into my bag after that or not.

But I had packed my own bag when we'd left the boat, and there hadn't been anything left in the cabin.

I went back into the bedroom and tipped the contents of my two suitcases onto the huge bed. I sifted through all the clothes, and dug into each compartment, but my phone wasn't there.

Okay, if I couldn't find it to charge, I'd have to use the phone downstairs. Thank goodness, I knew Sienna's number; I was hopeless with phone numbers but hers was an easy one to remember.

Gawd, if I'd lost my phone all my contacts would be gone. I opened the door and stepped out into the tiled corridor and headed for the staircase. The house was quiet and when I reached the bottom of the stairs, I paused unsure of where to go.

I tipped my head to the side; I could hear Rosco's voice coming from a room at the back of the villa.

I'd taken my shoes off upstairs and my bare feet made no sound as I walked on the cold tiles.

His voice got louder as I approached and for

a moment, I assumed he was on the phone, until I heard a female voice raised in anger. I walked slowly along the corridor, but I couldn't understand any of it as they spoke in rapid Italian.

But I did know that each speaker was angry.

I reached an open doorway and paused. Rosco was sitting at a desk and Davina was leaning over him, her pointed finger almost touching his face as she spat words at him. His face was flushed, and anger flashed from his eyes. I went to move back but he looked across at me, and his expression darkened further as he switched to English.

'I told you to stay upstairs until it was time for dinner.'

Anger rose up in my chest, and I strode into the room. 'I needed to speak to you. It's obviously a bad time. I'll wait in the hall until you have finished here.'

'No. Go back upstairs. I'll come up.'

I shook my head. 'No, I'll wait here. I wish to use the telephone.'

His mouth set in a straight line and he flicked a dismissive hand at Davina. *'Ne parleremo più tardi.'*

I looked around as I stepped into the room. Davina raised her eyebrows at me as she pushed past.

'I would like to use the telephone to call Sienna. My phone is missing. Have you seen it?'

'You are accusing me of taking it?'

I frowned. 'No, why would I think that?' Suspicion trickled through me.

Surely not?

'I don't know why you would think that. You have been difficult and irrational ever since we stepped onto the boat.'

My mouth dropped open and I took a step back. 'What?'

'Come upstairs. We will continue this conversation in private.' Rosco stood and came around the desk and took my arm quite roughly. This time I wasn't going to be manhandled, and I pulled away. As I strode ahead of him, and down the corridor towards the staircase, Davina walked past us looking quite smug.

By the time I reached the top of the stairs, he'd caught up to me.

'Marissa. Wait. I am sorry for snapping.' His hand touched my arm gently, but I shook it off. An apology wasn't going to cut it this time.

Walking into the bedroom, I turned to face him.

'Don't you ever speak to me like that again, or I'll be out of here like a shot.'

His face darkened as he looked past me. 'What is that?'

'What?' I turned.

'The clothes that I bought for you. You treat them like rubbish?'

'No, I haven't hung them up yet. I was looking for my phone. I would like to ring Sienna before she leaves Italy.'

'Why?'

My eyes widened as he approached me.

Chapter 10

Pippa: Pentecost Island

The opening date for the first stage of our eco-resort was six days away.

Six days! I smiled as I thought about it; that meant it was only five days until Rafe was due back on the island. I had missed him so much, and we had been so busy, but the time had flown. My life had changed so much over the past few months; I was happy and content and looking forward to the future. I think it was the first time for many years I had looked ahead rather than getting bogged down in my problems.

I jumped when Tam called out to me.

'Pip, stop mooning about and come and help me stow all these boxes.'

We'd been over to the mainland and picked up a huge supply of grog from the discount store at Airlie Beach. As I helped her move the boxes, so they were evenly balanced on each side of the boat, Tam giggled.

'Whatever you do, don't sink the boat on the way back. You'll poison the ocean with the amount of spirits we've got on board.'

'As long as we get enough customers to buy it, I'll be happy.' I said as I steered us across the passage between Hamo and our island.

'Trust me, I have no doubt they'll come,' Tam said. 'Kylie over at the tourism place said the word is out already.'

'Good.' I folded my arms. 'Because that order nearly broke us.'

Even Nell who was in charge of the accounts had protested at the amount of grog that Tam had ordered.

'Trust me, Pip,' Tam said with a smile. 'Really, I've sussed out the online community and the talk around the marinas, and a bar like this where they can anchor and come and socialise with other sailors is exactly what's needed. On the mainland they have marina fees, and if they moor out at the front of the town and pull up on shore in their tenders, they're only allowed to leave the tender there for a certain time. Our bar is not only going to offer whatever they want to drink—and excellent bar food—it's going to give them freedom to come and go as they please.'

'I hope you're right.'

'You watch, we'll have return business, and the word will spread.' Tam nodded as we stowed the last box below. 'Like I said, trust me.'

'Okay. I will.'

'Good.' She nudged me as we walked across the deck. 'Do you know how good it is to see you happy, Pip?'

I couldn't help my smile. 'Do you know how good it feels to be happy?' I replied.

'How long are you going to keep Rafe dangling? You haven't spent a night over there yet, have you?'

I pursed my lips at her in a mock stern look. 'That's my business.'

Tam shook her head with a laugh. 'Is this the same woman who came crying to Nell and me with the pink G-string story when Darren did the dirty?'

'Okay, fair enough. You two are my besties

and no, I haven't slept with him. I want to be completely sure I'm not in lust.' I gave her a rueful grin. 'Like I was every other time I got let down.'

'He's a pretty decent guy, Pip. You know what an excellent judge of character I am.'

I started the engine and Tam lifted the fenders as we backed out of the berth. She joined me at the helm when we were underway, and I picked up our conversation. 'I do, and you are.' I glanced sideways at her. 'We've been so busy this past ten days; we haven't had a chance to talk. So, speaking of your excellent character judgement, tell me what you think of Eliza.'

Tam leaned back on the padded seat behind her. 'She's an incredible worker.'

'Yep, I know that.'

'She's very . . . I'm not sure if the right word is shy . . . or private.'

'Do you trust her?' I asked as I swung the helm and headed towards our island.

'In what way? I don't think she's going to murder us in our beds or run off with the silver.'

I giggled. 'We don't have any silver. Do you think she's telling the truth?' I hadn't shared what I'd found out with Nell and Tam yet.

'No. There's something that doesn't ring true for me. She's full of stories about her childhood, but when I ask about recent years, she clams right up. And her accent changes, depending what she's talking about.'

'She wasn't over on Little Lindeman before you rescued her. Evie and I went over there, and no one knew her.'

'That doesn't surprise me.' Tam's expression was serious. 'But you know? Does it really matter? She's doing a damn fine job with us, and she's good company when we're working. When she lets go, she's got the best sense of humour.'

'You've nailed it there. "When she lets go." It's as though she's playing a role to me.'

Tam nodded. 'Yeah. Maybe she'll chill a bit the longer she stays, and you know, as long as she does the right thing by us, is it really our business?'

I shook my head. 'No, it's not. I'll let it go. She can stay as long as she wants. We've certainly got ahead of schedule with her working here. Speaking of which, have you thought any more about hiring staff? We'll need help in the bar once we open.'

'When it gets busy, you mean?'

'No, from the get-go. We've all got other jobs to do. We can't do our usual stuff and man it from lunchtime until closing.'

'I was going to leave it for a couple of weeks and just see how busy we were, but I guess you're right.'

'I think you should be there as the owner of the resort to make it personal and welcoming, but you'll also need someone.'

'I have to be there anyway under the Liquor Act. Nell has already read me the riot act on that. Several times.' I rolled my eyes. '"An individual licensee or approved manager must be present or reasonably available during ordinary trading hours."'

'I think seeing we're on an island you'll be reasonably available, but you do need a bar person.'

'Is this leading to something?' I asked suspiciously.

Tam had the grace to look embarrassed. 'One of my workmates at my old restaurant in Brisbane emailed me. She heard what we were doing up here and said if anything came up to let her know. She'd be perfect and she'd fit in with the rest of us.'

'Did I ever meet her?'

'Maybe. She was in the bar there. Long black hair past her waist, and she mixed the best cocktails ever.'

'I think I did. Maybe when I first moved to the Gold Coast. Was her name Cherry?'

Tam nodded. 'That's her. Cherry Chilcott.'

'So, is she available?'

'Between jobs, she told me.'

'Okay, tell her if she's interested to come up and we'll interview her. At least we know she's got her RSA.'

'*We'll* interview?' Tam said as I turned the boat into our bay. 'You're the boss.'

'Yep. And you're the hospitality person. You can pick your staff.'

Tam grinned. 'Thanks, boss.'

Chapter 11

Marissa: Tuscany

'Marissa! Where the hell have you been?' Sienna's voice screeched though the landline. Rosco was standing beside me in the study, so I was very conscious of what I said.

'On my honeymoon, you goose.'

'I've tried to call and call, and your phone kept going to voicemail. I was so worried I rang your parents.'

I swallowed. 'You rang my parents?' I half-turned my back so Rosco would get the hint and give me some privacy, but he crossed to his desk and sat down. I extended the cord on the phone—I couldn't believe the villa didn't have a cordless phone—and sat in a chair near the window. It had a high back and gave me a bit of privacy.

It bothered me that I felt the need for that. We'd been married three weeks now, and I was losing my confidence more each day. Up in the bedroom earlier when Rosco had snapped at me for emptying my suitcase on the bed, I had been taken aback, but he had got over it as quickly as his angry mood had come on. He had seen my uncertainty— at this stage it wasn't fear—as he'd approached me, but he'd put his arms around me and rubbed my back until I relaxed in his hold.

'I am sorry, my darling. I was angry because I argued with Davina. She did not follow my instructions while we were away, and I have lost a contract. I am so sorry that I snapped at you.'

I had leaned into him and buried my face

against his neck. The familiar smell of his aftershave and the warmth of his skin soothed me, but there was a part of me that couldn't let go of the fact that he was so moody and unpredictable. I was getting reluctant to show what I was thinking and say what I wanted.

'Do you forgive me?' His lips moved against my neck and his hands lifted my T-shirt, his fingers warm on my bare skin.

'Of course, I do.'

It didn't seem to matter to him that we fell onto the bed and were on top of all of the new clothes that he had seemed so worried about a few minutes earlier.

A very pleasant half hour ensued, and my confidence was restored. As we got out of the shower in the marble bathroom adjacent to our room a while later, Rosco flicked my wet hair with a finger.

'When you are dressed, come down to my study and I'll show you how to use the telephone.' He chuckled. 'You are in Italy now, my darling, and it is not as simple as you are used to.'

'Thank you,' I said as I towelled my hair dry. 'I guess I'll get used to things being different. I wonder where on earth my phone got to. I'll have a to get another one.'

My husband shook his head as he headed for the door. 'No. You don't need one.' As he'd shut the door behind him, I'd stared at it in disbelief.

I didn't need one?

The first chance I got, I'd be into the village we'd driven through on the way to the villa and I'd be buying a phone. No way was he going to tell me what I could or couldn't have.

I dressed quickly and hurried down to the study before he could change his mind about me making a call. The call went through to Sienna's mobile quickly and she answered on the first ring.

Gawd, she'd rung my oldies. I swallowed again. 'Um, what did they say?'

'They weren't home. I wasn't able to talk to them.'

Thank God.

'I lost my phone. At least I remembered your number. I've lost all the others. You know I don't even know the number for the manor.'

'Marissa, you are so hopeless. There's no need to worry. When you get a new one, use the same email to set up your phone and your contacts will all be in the cloud.'

'Oh, of course they will. I'd forgotten about that.'

'So, what did your parents think of Rosco?'

'We haven't been home yet. We went cruising in the Adriatic on Rosco's sailing boat instead.'

'Nice one. I bet you've got a tan. I'm going back home with one. I ended up going down to Sorrento after your wedding. I hooked up with a group. We had such a blast.'

'Sounds like fun,' I said.

'Where are you now? Any chance of catching up before I fly out?'

'We're back at Rosco's villa. I'll talk to him and see what our plans are, and I'll get back to you. I'm sure he'd love to see you too before you go back.'

A shadow fell between me and the window. I looked up. Rosco was shaking his head. He made a cutting motion telling me to end the call.

'Sienna, I have to go. I'll call you back in a while, okay?'

'Sure. It was great to hear from you. I have really been worried.'

'Why would that be?' I glanced up at Rosco. His face was set in a frown as he stared at me.

'I'll tell you when I see you. Okay, love, *Ciao.*'

The call ended and I handed the phone back to Rosco.

'I told you, you don't need a phone,' he said with an intent stare.

'I do.' I stood my ground. No one, not even my new husband was going to tell me what I could or couldn't do.

'You do not need a phone.' He reached out, and his fingers were cruel on my arm. 'Are you listening to me?'

I pulled away from him and tried to stay calm. 'I'm sorry, Rosco, but we are going to have to disagree on this. I need a phone, to get all of my contacts and numbers back. I also need a phone to maintain some of my independence.'

The look on his face that accompanied the short huff that came from his mouth was ugly.

'And you expect me to pay your bill, so you can keep in touch with all of your past friends? Oh no, no, no. You are my wife now, Marissa, and you will do as I say.'

'I will pay for it myself, and I will pay for the calls.' I took on a deep breath as I stared at him.

A smile crossed his face, but it wasn't pleasant and did not reassure me. 'And what money are you going to use for that? You will not work while you are married to me, Marissa. It is your job to be my wife.'

I kept my voice even. 'Yes, I am happy to be your wife and not work, if that is what you want, but I will also have a phone.'

'You no longer have your own money. You are dependent on me now. But do not worry. I will provide you with the best. All I expect in return is to have a beautiful wife in my house, and a wife to travel with me.'

I stared at him for a few seconds before I turned away. 'I will leave you to your work. I am going back to my room to have a rest for a while.'

That's what I told him, but what I intended was to get my purse and go down to the village and find somewhere to buy a phone.

Today.

His smile was strange as he pulled me close and kissed the top of my head as though I was a recalcitrant child. 'I will see you at dinner. Please wear the royal blue beaded dress.'

I managed to keep my expression neutral as I looked at Rosco and nodded briefly.

But my thoughts were dark and circling around my head.

What the fuck had I done?

Chapter 12

Pippa: Pentecost Island

Life on the island was getting frantic. With Eliza's help, the huts were almost complete, and as soon as the cladding went on, we were ready to fit them out with simple furniture and bedding.

The bar was opening in three days, and Tam was like a bear with a sore head. She was a perfectionist, and I had never seen anyone stress so much about bar food.

'All they'll want is a drink, Tam. Any extra is a bonus,' I said one afternoon as we stocked the bar with the bottles we'd bought on the mainland. Eliza was helping us carry the boxes down and she nodded.

'Pippa is right, Tam. Any food to soak up the alcohol will be welcome. You could put out potato crisps and a sailor would be happy.'

Tam shook her head with a mutinous look on her face. 'There will be no potato crisps from my kitchen. Pip, I want you to look at the menu for the bar food and approve it before I go ahead.'

'Why?' I said as I decided what colour bottles to put together on the shelf.

'Because you're the boss. Someone has to sign off on what I propose.'

'Nope.' I shook my head. 'That's your department, and I give you full responsibility. It's called trust, Tam. I don't look over Nell's shoulder at the spreadsheets and the software, and I don't tell Evie what plants to buy. So just like that, I don't pretend to know what bar food you're going to make to go with all these pretty drinks.' I put the blue bottle next to the red one and stood back and admired my handiwork. We had designed the bar with a nautical theme—duh, of course we did, we were on an island—and nets and knotted ropes were draped behind the bar. There were six high stools along the front of the wooden bar top and a scattering of tables and chairs undercover on the paved area. The bar had no walls and the view from every stool and chair out over our bay was superb and unhindered. On a nice day we'd move the tables out onto the sand.

Tam groaned. 'Are you sure?'

I walked over and put my hands on her shoulders. 'Of course, I'm sure. Um, how long have we known each other?'

'A bloody long time,' she replied with a frown.

'And in that twenty something years, you have never let me down, so why would you do it now? This bar is going to be a rip-roaring success, and the word about your food will spread from one end of the islands to the other. And wait until the restaurant gets going. Your food will bring them from further afield.'

Tam finally smiled. 'It will be good, won't it?'

'Yep. Ma Carmichael's is going to be the best place in the islands to stay and to dine.'

Eliza emptied the bottles from the last carton and sat them on the bar before she turned to us. 'Have you ever thought of having a theme here?'

'What do you mean by a theme?' I asked.

'Maybe theme isn't the right word. I've done a bit of travelling around the world, and there were many places that were booked out for months ahead. Some places specialised in weddings, and others in fishing charters.'

'We're going down the eco-resort path, but I'd love to hear about what you've seen,' I said. It was unusual for Eliza to initiate a conversation and share anything about herself and her recent life.

She pulled out a chair and turned it around and straddled it with her arms along the back.

I pulled out a chair and sat facing her. 'I like this conversation. Tam, I think you should whip up a cocktail for us and we'll throw around some ideas. Eliza, hold those thoughts. I'll go and find Evie and Nell.'

Evie had just come in from the vegetable garden and headed straight down to the bar, but it took me a few minutes to entice Nell away from her desk.

'Come on, Nell. You need some down time.' She had been working on projections and spreadsheets for the past week. Like Tam as our opening approached, Nell was getting nervous. My calm was out of character and I realised what a long way I'd come.

'Thanks, Aunty Vi.' I looked up at the sky as I murmured under my breath. I could only hope she was up there looking down on us and smiling. It had taken me a long time to come to terms with death after I had lost my parents at such a young age, but again, Aunty Vi had played a big part in teaching me acceptance.

'I'm having trouble with the backup system,' Nell said as she followed me down the stairs.

'Step away from it for a while. It could be the internet connection. My phone has been dodgy all day. When Rafe called this morning, it kept dropping out.' He'd rung me twice a day for the last two weeks and I was so looking forward to his return. Being apart had made me realise it was time to take our relationship to the next level.

I was ready. I'd learned to trust again.

Nell nodded. 'It could be. I'm going to have to go to a hard disk backup as well as the cloud. Is that okay with you?'

'That's your baby, Nell. You're the boss.' I grinned. 'I've just had the same conversation with Tam. And Eliza has come up with some ideas. That's why I want us all together.'

'Okay, give me five minutes.'

Ten minutes later I stopped at the end of the path where Evie had created a small garden edged with logs. Already some of her tropical plants had flowered and were providing a pretty show.

Ahead of Nell and I was the most incredible palette of colours as the sun dipped towards the water. A lone sailing boat was the only thing between the shore and the magnificent sky, the headsail billowing in the afternoon wind; a backdrop of burnt orange cloud edged with silver contrasted with the while sail and the silvery-blue water the boat glided over.

'Thank you, Pip.' Nell's voice was hushed. 'Thank you for sharing your island with us.'

I linked my arm through hers as we walked across the sand to the bar. 'Thank you for being here. I think we've got a pretty tight group here now. I appreciate you all.'

'Even Eliza?' she asked quietly.

'Yes, she's a hard worker. Whatever secrets she holds are her business. And I've got to like her more each day.'

'Good. I think she is a great addition to the team. And how gorgeous, is she? She could have been a model.'

'She can turn her hand to anything, that's for sure. Plus, she's got some great ideas. That's why I want everyone down here to listen now.'

When we reached the edge of the open space of the bar, I stood back and looked at it. The girls had shelved the rest of the bottles and hung a row of champagne flutes along the two stainless steel wires that Eliza had suggested would be perfect for hanging glasses.

'I saw it up in Cairns,' she'd said the other day. 'Cheap, simple and effective.'

I picked up the wire when we were over on the mainland, along with a list of other bits and pieces that Eliza had suggested. What she had done with some cheap fittings and the contents of our toolbox amazed me.

Yes, she was a great asset to our team, and I wanted her to stay.

Tam was shaking a silver cocktail shaker with flair and did a fancy manoeuvre before she lifted it and poured a fluffy blue concoction into the cocktail glasses lined up on the burnished timber bar top—another of Eliza's creations in the past week. That had saved me a fortune.

'That looks interesting it. What are we having?'

Tam grinned at me. 'We're starting with the PI Special.'

'Ah. Let me guess. Pentecost Island?' I reached for it to take a sip, but she grabbed the glass before my hand reached it. 'Okay, and what do you mean by starting with,' I asked.

Tam came out from behind the bar, placed the five glasses on a tray and carried them over to the table where the others were sitting. 'I'm a chef, not a bar person, so I need to practise my cocktails on some volunteers.' She passed the glasses around the table, and I sat down in one of the vacant chairs.

'Okay, first sip and an immediate ranking out of ten, please ladies,' Tam said.

We all obliged.

'Yum, what's in that?' Nell asked. 'I'll give it a ten.'

'Vodka, coconut rum, blue curacao, pineapple juice, lemon soda, and a twist of lime.'

'Wow, that's some hangover material.' Eliza took another sip and then smiled. 'But I can live with that. A ten from me too.'

Evie nodded. 'And me.'

'Pip?' Tam looked at me anxiously.

I slowly lifted the glass and took another sip as I looked at the women sitting around the table. Contentment filled me; I felt comfortable with all of them and would never stop appreciating the effort they were all making to help me achieve my dream.

'Not a ten.' I shook my head and drained the

glass to everyone's astonishment. 'That's an eleven from me.'

By Tam's third creation—a pink one to follow the blue and the yellow—we were all getting mellow, if not a little tipsy.

I held up my hand. 'We need to slow down and listen to Eliza's idea. Finish what you started to tell us before.'

She put her glass down and fiddled nervously with the paper straw. 'Well, I was wondering if you might have already considered this. I would suggest that the island and the house is the perfect location for an exclusive day spa.'

I tipped my head to the side as I watched her. Sometimes Eliza's speech was very formal, and sometimes her Kiwi accent was strong, and other times it seemed to be blended with something else. All part of her mystery package.

She held my gaze aware of my scrutiny. 'I was looking at the layout of the house the other afternoon and had an idea. If everyone moved into the rooms at the back, you could open up the four front rooms, and put in bigger windows opening out onto the verandah and that gorgeous view. You could have a variety of exclusive treatments, with natural products to fit in with the theme of your eco-resort.'

I nodded slowly as I considered the idea. 'We did discuss something on a smaller scale before we even moved here. It would cost a lot to make the structural changes to the house though.'

'I can do that,' Eliza said.

I raised my eyebrows. One thing she didn't lack was confidence in her work.

'And what about beauty therapists or

whatever it is they're called these days?' Tam said. 'Would it be hard to get someone to come to the island? We're pretty isolated out here.'

'If you put out what you want to the universe, you will get what you want.' Eliza's voice seemed deeper and her words surprised me. I didn't see her as a New Age type of person.

'You think it's that easy?' I tried not to be too cynical.

'Can you visualise it?' she asked. 'Close your eyes, Pippa. Imagine a room, a peaceful room with royal blue curtains blowing in the gentle breeze of the bay. Soft pipe music drifts from the room. Two women sit on the verandah with fruit juice waiting for their treatments. Calm and serenity surround them.'

Damn, I could see it. My interest flared.

'I have a friend who might be interested in working here,' Eliza added. 'She's a qualified therapist.'

'I'm loving the sound of this,' Evie said with a grin. 'Could staff book in?'

'What do you think, Nell? Do you have time to do a feasibility study?' My practical side chimed in despite the two and half cocktails.

Nell's chuckle belied her always-serious expression. 'I can make time.'

'Excellent. Thank you, Eliza. It's this hive mind that's going to make our resort a success.'

Eliza beamed as she reached for her drink. 'Thank you for letting me be a part of it. The more I can help, the less of an intruder I feel.' She stared past me and her eyes narrowed.

I turned to see what she was looking at. The sailing boat I had admired when Nell and I had walked down from the house was coming into our bay. I stood and walked down to the sand and as I watched, surprise filled me. The skipper headed directly to the channel between the coral heads and within minutes was safely in our bay.

'He's done that before.' Tam came to stand beside me.

'Apparently.' I looked more closely at the boat. It was an old white sloop; she had graceful lines but had seen some wear and tear. The skipper brought her right into the sand, jumped over the front and tied the bow onto two palm trees that were near the water's edge. A tall man in white shorts and a navy-blue T-shirt strolled up the beach towards us.

I turned around. 'Evie, isn't that your French friend from Hamo the other day? You said you'd invited him, but he's arrived a bit early.'

Chair legs scraped on the pavers that we'd laid for the bar floor as Eliza stood.

'I have some emails to send to my family. Thanks for the cocktails, Tam. I'll see you all in the morning.' She turned quickly and walked past the bar, but Tam called after her.

'What about dinner?'

Eliza waved her hand and her voice was short. 'No thanks. I'm not hungry.' She was out of sight in seconds.

Evie hurried down to meet the man who was tying off his boat, and I followed.

'You've done that before,' I said. 'You knew where to find the channel, especially as it's almost dark.'

'I do.' He nodded and held out his hand. '*Bon soir*. I am Phillipe Renton. I hope it is allowable for me to moor here for tonight. And yes, I was in the Whitsundays about eight years ago, and learned about your channel that the Americans made in the Second World War. There's another one over at Happy Bay on Palm Island, but not many sailors knew about this one when I was here last time.'

My eyes widened. 'The Second World War? I didn't know about them being on the island.'

Phillipe walked up the beach behind us. 'This must be the bar that Evie told me about. And I heard that you are planning a restaurant also?' His accent was divine, and I could see Evie hanging off his every word.

'Not yet, but we will. And yes, you are more than welcome to moor here for the night. Oh, and I'm Pippa.'

'Your bay is not in the *One Hundred Magic Miles* book, so I wasn't sure if it was acceptable to moor in the bay.'

'What book is that? I asked as we reached the bar.

'It's the bible for sailors in the Whitsundays, and it lists the anchorages and moorings for all of the bays and resorts.' He stood back to allow Evie and I to go in first.

'I think the tourism girls on the mainland told me about it. And as you are our first visitor, there will be no charge. We are not quite open for business. We're almost ready.'

'Three more days,' Tam said. 'But we have drinks in the fridge here. What would you like?'

Jiminy's best mate, Taj, who lived on Hamilton Island was an electrician, and he'd spent a day over here running the power down to the bar.

We'd decided to have LED lights in the huts, but there was a charging station with six double power points on a bench at the far side of the bar.

'A cold beer would be excellent, but I insist on paying for it, and for my mooring too.'

I introduced Tam and Nell and he shook their hands in turn.

'*Enchanté.*' His voice was deep and accented, and I would swear I saw the three girls swoon. But not me; even though he was a honey, my heart was firmly in Rafe's safekeeping.

'This looks very good.' Philippe looked around. 'You've changed it a lot. The last time I was here this was an old boatshed.'

'Yes, the only things we kept were the original timber posts,' I said. 'Did you meet the owner when you were here?'

'I did. She was a delightful woman. I assume she's passed on for you to be developing a resort.'

'Yes, she was my mother's aunt. We all live up in the old house now. We're slowly doing it up.'

His gaze flicked over to the huts. Eliza and Evie had the frames finished and we were waiting for Bunnings to call to say the cladding was in. I was hoping to pick it up when Rafe flew into the mainland airport the day after tomorrow. He'd changed his flight destination especially so it would save me an extra trip over to the mainland.

'We?'

'There's five of us working here at the moment. Eliza is back at the house. Friends as well as staff. I have a good team.'

'I had heard on the sailing grapevine that there was a tribe of Amazons doing it all themselves on this island. I guess they were referring to you and your team.' He looked suitably impressed and smiled as he took the glass of beer from Tam. 'Thank you. I'll have to spread the word for you.'

'Best form of advertising,' I said. 'But leave it for a few days. The official opening is next weekend.

'Would you like another drink, Pip?' Tam asked from behind the bar.

'Just a soda, thanks.' I'd been getting tipsy on her potent cocktails and I didn't want the sailing grapevine to put about that we were a party island. 'Then I've got some work to do, but you three are on your own time now, so please keep Phillipe company.'

Tam shot me a look telling me she understood where I was coming from. Evie smiled and Nell looked impatient. I knew she'd be anxious to get back to her files. She worked way too hard.

I finished my soda and stood. 'Because you insist on paying for your mooring, I'll insist that you join us for breakfast on the house verandah in the morning. I want to hear all about this war channel dredging. I'd always assumed it was natural.'

'That would be my pleasure.' He stood when I pushed my chair in. Nell was right behind me as I headed for the beach.

'See you tomorrow,' she said with a wave.

I grinned as we walked back to the house. 'I think both Tam and Evie have fallen under the spell of our first guest.'

'Nope. Not Tam,' Nell said. 'She's just being polite.'

'Do you know what happened with Chad?' I

asked curiously. 'I know it was a messy break up, and I don't think she's been out with anyone since then.'

'All I know is Chad broke her heart. I don't think she's ever got over him. Last I heard he was marrying some girl from Sydney.'

'Maybe a hot French dude is just what she needs.'

'Probably, but I think Evie's got her eye out there, don't you?'

'Seemed to have.' We climbed up the steps and went inside; the house was in darkness and there was no sign of Eliza. I flicked the lights on. 'I'm going to cook some toast and work on a flyer to take over to the mainland on Tuesday. Is the printer working?'

She nodded glumly. 'It's about the only thing that is. I'm going to try and get it all sorted tonight. Throw a couple of pieces of toast in for me too, please. I need something to soak up those cocktails and clear my head.

It might have been the residual effect of the cocktail, but a huge surge of happiness went through me. I grabbed both Nell's hands. 'This is going to be *so* good, isn't it?'

Her smile was wide. 'It already is good. I'm very happy working here. Even when I struggle with the IT.'

'And I'm happy to have such fantastic friends.'

'Don't forget that gorgeous man who's almost on his way back to you. Have you heard from him?' She laughed and said. 'Okay, silly question. Of course, you have.' After a moment her expression grew serious. 'Are you okay with this,

Pip? I mean, I think Rafe is a great guy, but I—and Tam—well, we don't want to see you hurt. There's been a lot of changes for you in the past few months.'

'Oh, Nell.' I reached out and hugged her. 'You know I love you both for worrying about me. But, honestly? I don't think I've ever been this happy—or so sure of anything in my life before. Rafe is the man for me, and I know he feels the same way. I would trust him with my life.'

'That's a sweeping statement.' The cynical voice came from behind me and I turned. Eliza stood in the dark hall and had obviously been listening to our conversation without making herself known.

'It might be,' I said rather tersely. 'But it's the way I feel.'

'Just be careful.' Eliza's voice was soft and as she stepped out into the light, I could see her face was pale.

'Don't worry, I am. We are. We've all been hurt at one time or another and we know the way it can be.' I glanced at Nell. I knew she'd had a bad experience at uni and as far as I knew she'd never gone out with a guy since. 'Sounds like you're part of the club too.'

I thought of the ring that Eliza had in her safekeeping.

'The club?'

'The been-dumped club.' I said. 'A shame our visitor interrupted us, we could have had a good girls' night on the cocktails and a natter.'

'Is he still down there?' Her voice was still quiet as she went into the kitchen and filled the jug.

'Evie and Tam are keeping him entertained.

He's already said he'll recommend our place.'

'Your place. I just work here.'

She was in a strange mood.

'I like to think it's a team effort,' I said as I reached for three mugs. 'You might have only been here a couple of weeks, Eliza, but I'd like you to know I do appreciate how hard you've been working. And your ideas. I hope you'll stay with us for a while before you move on.'

'I'll see. It depends on a few things.' Eliza jumped as the kettle gave its shrill whistle.

'Fair enough. Tea or coffee, Nell?' I asked.

'Coffee please. I'm going to work until late.'

I looked after Eliza thoughtfully as she took her coffee back to her room. I noticed the light was still shining under her door when I went to bed well after midnight.

Chapter 13

Marissa: Tuscany

Staying in Rosco's villa—I still couldn't think of it as home—before we went to visit my family, was both a good and bad thing. It gave me more of an idea of what my life was going to be like as Rosco worked in his study with Davina each day before he came up to see me in the afternoon to tell me what he would like me to wear for dinner. It also gave me a yardstick with which to compare my family home. Meynell Manor certainly didn't measure up to this luxurious villa, and I worried about Rosco's reaction when we arrived.

Every day I wondered why he had married me, and every night, my doubts fled as he told me— and showed me how much he loved me.

I'd had no contact with anyone apart from my husband, and the cow who'd worked with him since we'd arrived. I was beginning to loathe Davina. The way she looked at me made me feel uncomfortable, and a couple of times when Rosco had not been around, she had called me Celeste.

'My name is Marissa,' I informed her coldly.

'Oh. So it is,' she said with a strange smile. 'I do get you all mixed up.'

I had no idea what she meant, and I wasn't sure whether to ask Rosco or not. It really bothered me how much my confidence was disappearing. Maybe it was marriage that did that to you. All of a sudden, you were one of a pair and had to think about another person's happiness. I didn't like upsetting him.

Back in those early weeks, I didn't realise that my reaction was a form of self-protection. Sure, Rosco might have been moody, but he smothered me with love when he was out of his study. So much that at times, I felt like a princess.

Before I had a chance to walk to the village alone, he took me for a walk one afternoon and we'd had a drink at a small café before we'd come back to the villa for dinner. The visit to the village showed me I would be wasting my time if I thought I could get a phone there. There was nothing there apart from medieval buildings, a lace shop, a leather shop and a couple of outdoor bars.

There was a cook and a guy to look after Rosco's cellar, so I was at a loss to understand what the fuss about me not being able to cook was all about.

When we were in England, I fully intended getting a phone. I was going to go stir crazy not talking to any of my friends. Even talking to my two bitch sisters would be better than this quiet life.

'What are you thinking about, my love?'

I jumped as Rosco sat next to me. 'Oh, nothing much,' I lied.

'I have something to tell you that I think will bring your smile back. I haven't seen it much these past two weeks.' His words held a note of criticism. 'Don't you love my home?'

'I've been adjusting,' I said slowly, then immediately worried that I had said the wrong thing.

Where had that confident, sassy person I had been six weeks ago disappeared to?

The woman who had set out on an adventure

with her best friend.

'As long as you don't change your mind.'

'Change my mind?'

'About being my wife.'

I shook my head quickly, very pleased that he couldn't read my thoughts. 'Of course not. I am just getting used to living—' I bit my words off before I put my foot in it. 'Living in a beautiful villa and getting to know the countryside and the customs,' I finished off feebly.

'If you ever did change your mind, I would not allow you to leave, you know. You are my wife now. And you will be forever.'

I reached out and took his face between my hands. His skin was smooth beneath my fingers and I noticed his hair was wet. He had showered and shaved even though it was only mid-afternoon.

'Don't even think that. I love you Rosco, and you are my husband. I will adjust.'

'You shouldn't have to make an effort to adjust,' he said coldly.

'I'm trying. But you have to understand. I was someone who went to work every day, and I have to get used to this freedom in my days.'

His face split into a sudden smile, at odds with the tone of his voice a minute ago.

'What would you say if I told you I had bought tickets to fly to London tomorrow. It is past time that I met your parents.'

Sweet relief flooded through me. 'Really?' Despite my determination to be reserved, I almost squealed the words.

'Yes, really.' Rosco put his arms around me and rested his chin on the top of my head. When he held me all my doubts fled, and I knew I had to make more of an effort to be happy here.

'Tomorrow. We will leave after breakfast.' He pulled me closer and it was hard to breathe. 'But tonight, we have a guest for dinner. Please wear the beige silk dress.'

I nodded. As much as I hated him telling me what to wear nothing was going to interfere with my happiness tonight.

We were going home.

Dinner was unpleasant, and my happy mood didn't last long. As well as Ren—the yachtsman I had met on our honeymoon, who Rosco had apparently recently conducted business with—the cow, Davina, made up the numbers. She was also dressed in silk, but the yellow made her olive skin look puce.

What was happening to me? I was changing into a person I sometimes didn't like very much. I swallowed and tried to join in the conversation.

My grasp of Italian was improving, but I was grateful to Ren, who switched to English, every time Davina chattered on in staccato speed dialect.

'Are you enjoying the countryside?' he asked me. 'Or would you rather be living on Rosco's boat?'

I tipped my head to the side, conscious of Rosco's interest in my answer. Davina's eyes glittered as Ren took his attention from her.

'I enjoy both,' I said carefully.

Ren turned to my husband. 'Are you taking any trips this winter?'

'Quite possibly. What do you suggest?'

'I spent the winter in the South Pacific six years ago. It was one of the most beautiful places I have been, and I intend going back one winter. The Whitsunday Islands.'

I carefully sliced the meat on my plate before looking across the table at him. 'I was under the impression that you lived on your boat, Ren.'

He laughed and held my gaze. I looked down, again conscious of Rosco's eyes on me. He didn't look happy and a small spurt of anger played havoc with my digestion.

'I wish that I could live on the sea. I spend as much time as I can on the water, but my business takes me away.'

I nodded and focused on my food.

'One day I will retire and travel the seven seas.'

Rosco's laugh was harsh. 'I will believe that only when I see it. You love making money too much, my friend.'

I thought that was a very rude comment, and Davina chimed in, in Italian, obviously backing him up.

The atmosphere was quite tense for a while, and the only noise was the clinking of cutlery on the fine china.

Finally, when we finished our coffee, Rosco stood. 'I have some business to conduct with Ren before he leaves. Good night, my dear.'

I felt like a child banished to bed, and I protested. 'I am quite happy to wait here until you come up too.'

Davina looked gleeful, and Ren looked embarrassed as Rosco snapped at me. 'Do as I say.'

To my disgust, I did as I was told, but I was aware of sympathy—and perhaps concern—in Ren's eyes as I walked up the wide staircase.

If I'd thought dinner was unpleasant, the treatment that I received when Rosco finally came to our bed, reeking of brandy was even worse. I pretended to be asleep as he pinned me to the bed and put his face against mine. 'I saw the way you looked at my friend. And so did Davina and of course, Ren. Don't you ever embarrass me like that again, Marissa.'

I rolled away from him and sat up. 'You are drunk,' I said coldly. 'I will ignore the rubbish that you are saying.'

I cringed as he raised his hand to me. I pulled my head back as his hand slapped against my cheek. If I hadn't have moved, it would have been a stinging blow, but it just glanced across my cheek.

I scurried across the bed, and climbed out before he could reach me, unable to process that he had tried to hit me. 'How dare you!'

I ran across the room and pushed open the door to the en suite bathroom, as Rosco came after me. The heavy door had a lock on it, and I pushed the door shut and flicked the lock over. I turned my back and leaned against the door, my knees shaking so much I was barely able to stand. I slid down the door and sat on the cold tiles and put my hand over my eyes.

'*Bella*, I am so sorry. Please forgive me. Please come out. I should not have done that.'

I shook my head from side to side. No, he most certainly shouldn't have done that.

I sat there trying to figure out what to do, until the first glimmer of dawn crept through the window.

When I unlocked the door an hour later, I pushed it open as quietly as I could. Before I could take a step, I was taken in a strong hold as Rosco pulled me to him. He put his face against mine and I was taken aback to feel his cheek damp against mine.

His voice broke and his words shook as he begged me to forgive him. 'I will not drink again. I am sorry. I was drunk and out of control. I am so, so sorry, my darling. Will you please forgive me? I will do anything. Buy you anything you want. I will take you anywhere you want to go. Just please forgive me and tell me you love me.'

I had stopped shaking finally, and the warmth of his skin against mine was soothing. I lowered my head and rested my face in the hollow of his neck as his tears continued to splash onto my skin. 'Do I have your word you will never raise your hand to me again?'

'Of course. I will swear it on our family bible.'

'And that you will never speak to me like that again? Either in private, or in front of people?'

'I swear. I love you, Marissa. I could not bear to lose you.'

'And you will buy me a phone so that I can

have contact with my friends and family without having to ask your permission.' I felt him tense against me, but he nodded. 'Of course, I was going to get you one and surprise you as soon as we got to Rome.' His words vibrated against my cheek. 'I love having you as my wife, and I will do anything to keep you. Will you promise me you won't leave me?'

I nodded slowly. 'I promise.'

It was a promise that I would find very hard to keep over the following months.

Chapter 14

Pippa: Pentecost Island

I was up early the next morning knowing Tam would be in the kitchen at dawn. If our first official guest was coming for breakfast, she would be pulling out all stops.

I was right; as I walked towards the kitchen, a tempting aroma tickled my nose and my stomach gurgled in anticipation. Tam was singing quietly as she stood at the stove and I smiled. She was in the full getup; the high collared white shirt was tucked into the black and white checked chef trousers, and her hair was pulled back under a white bandana.

'I'm impressed.' I said as I headed for the coffee machine.

'None of us had dinner last night so I thought I'd do the full works. When you pour your coffee can you help me move that long table out to the verandah, please? I'm going to set up a hot and cold buffet.'

I walked over and looked over her shoulder. She had three pots bubbling on the stove. 'Jeez, what time did you get up?'

Her grin was cheeky. 'I was too pumped after we'd had a few more drinks. I didn't.'

'Didn't go to bed? You're mad, woman.'

'Nuh. I'm excited. This is getting very real, Pip. I want it to be perfect.'

'It smells pretty damn perfect to me. We'll clean up after we eat, and you can go to bed.'

Another grin. 'I was counting on that.'

I leaned back on the bench and sipped my

coffee. 'Did you get in touch with your friend who you suggested for the bar?'

'Yes, I emailed the other night, but she hasn't replied yet. She might be away.'

'Before we have our first bookings for the huts, we're going to have to get some wait staff.' I took another sip and frowned. 'It's a hard call. We're a bit isolated, there's no boat service from Hamo to here, and we really don't want *every* staff member living on site just yet.'

'It is a bit tricky. Get Nell onto it. She thinks outside the square.' Tam leaned over and turned on the new grill we'd installed, and then opened the oven a crack and nodded. A mouth-watering aroma immediately filled the kitchen.

'Bread?' I almost moaned. 'You've cooked fresh bread too?'

'I have. Now finish that coffee and help me get set up. Phillipe said he'd come over about seven-thirty. He was going to head off today, but I think Evie talked him into staying in the bay for a few days. He was talking about going over to Indian Head to look at the summit. He's talking about climbing it.'

'That's a big climb. He'd have to start early. Seems like a nice guy.' I rinsed my mug.

'It would be a lonely life living on a boat by yourself though. I couldn't do it, could you?' Tam said.

'Never know until you try it.'

As we moved the table out to the verandah, Tam stopped in the doorway. 'I have an idea. What about Jiminy?'

'What about him?'

'Didn't he say that he was getting less work?

Instead of you running over to the island and picking up guests, why don't you ask him if he would start a service? It could be lucrative for him, and you would save time and money. He could also ferry staff over for day shifts.'

I nodded. 'That's not a bad idea. I'll swing into Hamo and see him on the way to the mainland on Wednesday. You're certainly on fire this morning.'

By seven-thirty the buffet table was loaded with cereal and the freshly baked bread. Two pitchers of milk sat side by side, with a jug of pineapple juice next to a platter of fresh fruit. Tam had even found time to pick some hibiscus flowers for decoration.

'I didn't realise you'd done so much shopping,' I said.

'I've been stocking up every time we go over to Hamo. Evie took me over the other day too.' Tam smoothed her hands down the front of her trousers. 'Here comes our guest, now. You can do the meet and greet.' She flashed me another grin. 'I'm just the kitchen staff.'

I rolled my eyes. 'Go on then. Get back to the stove, cook.'

'Chef, please. He looks like a fried egg man to me. What do you think?'

'Nuh, five bucks says poached,' I said with a laugh.

I went to the steps and waited for Phillipe to cross the lawn. Evie had worked magic with the old garden already. She had salvaged a lot of plants that had been hidden by overgrowth and had edged the gardens with more small logs she'd carted from the forest. The lawn was lush and green, and she had cleared around the large paving stones that had been there since I was a child.

'*Bonjour,* Phillipe. Welcome to Ma Carmichael's.'

He held out his hand and took mine in a half shake, half squeeze. 'Good morning, Pippa.'

I led him to the table we had set and gestured for him to take the chair that gave him a view of the bay to one side and the house on the other.

He waited for me to sit first and then looked out over the garden. 'This is delightful. Thank you for allowing me to be here.'

'Our pleasure. It's special to me knowing that you were here when my aunt was here.

His smile was gentle. 'We sat on those steps and she made me a cup of strong Australian tea. I was polite but I have never tried it since.'

I laughed. 'Aunt Vi loved her cuppa strong enough to stand a spoon in it. I'll get you a coffee.'

Before I could move, Tam appeared with the coffee pot.

'Good morning. Coffee?'

Philippe nodded. '*Merci.* There is a delectable smell coming from the kitchen.'

How would you like your eggs?' she asked.

'Scrambled, please, he said.

Tam and I exchanged an amused look as she put the pot on the table and disappeared back into the kitchen.

'Tam's been busy. I'd say we're in for a

feast. Now tell me about the channel to the bay you mentioned last night.'

Phillipe leaned forward and picked up his coffee. 'In World War Two the US servicemen used to come to the islands for R and R. Your aunt told me how they discovered Pentecost Island, and they organised to have a channel blasted so they could get here quickly and easily. Apparently, her father was very welcoming, and they wanted to pay him back for his hospitality.'

'Wow, I never knew that. There is so much I don't know about the island, or her family for that matter. We lost so much history when she passed away.' I stared out over the bay imagining what it would have been like back in the war. 'Aunty Vi must have been a child then.'

'She said she was about ten at the end of the war.'

I nodded. 'That would be about right. Thank you, Phillipe, it means a lot to me to hear some island history'

Tam's head appeared around the kitchen door. 'I'm putting the eggs on now, Pip, if you'd like to call the girls.'

As I stood, the door at the end of the verandah opened with a loud creak. Phillipe looked up and his mouth dropped open. Eliza was walking towards us, her attention on her phone. Phillipe's eyes widened, and his mouth opened.

I moved away from the table and Eliza looked up. 'I've had a reply from my—' She stopped when she noticed Phillipe sitting at the table.

I watched curiously as the colour leached from her face and she stopped. She stared at Phillipe for a moment, and her phone slipped from her hands.

She bent to pick it up. 'Oh, I'm . . . er . . . sorry. I didn't realise that we had company.' Turning swiftly, she took a step back towards the door.

'Wait.' Philippe shot to his feet. 'Please. Ma—' He shook his head and stopped talking, his eyes fixed on Eliza.

Eliza shook her head and quickly disappeared through the door.

I looked from the closed door to Phillipe. He looked like he'd seen a ghost.

Picking up the coffee pot, I topped up his cup.

He picked it up and I noticed his hand was shaking. 'What is her name? Please?'

'Eliza.'

'She is another friend of yours?'

'She is becoming one.' I was intrigued by his reaction. Eliza was very beautiful, but she downplayed it in the way she dressed and the messy way her short dark curls framed her face. 'She's only been with us for a short while.'

'How long?' His words held urgency.

'About three weeks now. Why do you ask?'

'She looks very much like someone I know. I mean, someone I knew. She died a few months ago.' His face was still pale.

'I'm sorry to hear that.'

He drained his coffee and I topped it up again.

'What is her whole name? Do you know where she is from?' He fired the questions at me.

'Eliza Pengelly. From New Zealand.'

He shook his head. 'I thought perhaps Marissa may have had a sister. They could almost be doubles, but she was English. I'm sorry, I am being very rude.'

'It's fine. They say we all have a *doppelganger* somewhere in the world. Eliza is a private person. I'm sorry to hear about your friend.' I reached over and squeezed his hand.

Eliza's fast disappearance had me curious. I had seen the look of terror on her face when she had first seen Phillipe, but she had masked it very quickly. I also remembered how she had disappeared as soon as his boat had appeared in the bay yesterday.

Curiouser and curiouser.

Nell and Evie surfaced and sat at the table beside us. Phillipe had recovered his equilibrium, but he was quiet. Evie tried to get him talking but soon gave up as he focused on eating the laden plate that Tam brought out.

By the time we had all eaten, there was still no sign of Eliza, although Phillipe kept glancing towards the closed door. Eventually he stood and I pushed my chair back.

'Thank you for breakfast,' he said. 'Please tell Tam it was most enjoyable.' He still seemed preoccupied.

'I'll walk you back to the beach. I hear you're thinking of going to Indian Head today?'

'Perhaps. Is it acceptable if I stay moored in your bay for a few days? I will pay of course. I would like to climb the summit one day.'

'Yes, we would be pleased to have you stay.' I knew I would, but I wondered about Eliza's reaction. I was going to search her out as soon as

Phillipe was back on his boat. I'd accepted her secrecy since she'd arrived, but if there was something that was going to impact on our guests, I wanted to know what it was.

The sun was high, and the day was promising to be a beauty. A few sails dotted the passage, the wind filling them as the yachts scooted along at a good speed. Philippe's boat showed its age in the daytime.

He saw me looking and gave me his first smile for a while. 'I know she looks tired, but she is a solid boat. She has taken me all around the world.'

'As long as she floats.' I cleared my throat. 'May I ask what happened to your friend?'

He stared out over the bay. 'Marissa was married to a business colleague of mine. She wasn't a very close friend. I only met her a few times, but there was something about her . . .' He swallowed. 'I caught up with them in Cairns, and we had dinner on Rosco's boat one night. I set off to the south, and he called me distraught two days later. Marissa drowned one night when they were out near Green Island.'

'Oh, I'm sorry. That is very sad. No wonder you looked so shocked when you saw someone who looked like her.'

'Yes, but now that I think about it, they are different. Your Eliza is taller and more, how do you say, slight, I think, and her hair is dark. Marissa's hair was long and blonde. She was very beautiful.' He almost seemed to be talking to himself. 'Rosco's wives were both very beautiful.'

'Both?'

'Yes, sadly his first wife was killed in a car accident.'

'Oh, such tragedy. I'm sorry you've had a sad morning.'

'Thank you for listening and thank you again for breakfast. I'm going to go and get some exercise.'

'I hope you do stay a few days. My partner will be home from Europe this week, and you will have some male company. Anyway, have a good day. Time for me to head to work. I'll see you later, Phillipe.'

He nodded, and his smile was sad.

I headed back to the house: I wanted to have a chat with Eliza.

Chapter 15

Marissa

The visit home was not what you'd call a happy event. Dad was okay about our marriage, but I could see the hurt lurking beneath his usual jovial exterior. My mother's reaction was as I'd expected; she was in awe of Rosco, his charm—he really turned it on—and his obvious wealth. He seemed to feel the need to tell them about his business, his villa, his boat—boats—yet little about himself.

I guess I was still angry with him and I had pretty much shut down. I hated being home. Being in the light and airy villa for the past couple of weeks, and before that living on the boat, made our ancestral home seem darker and dingier than it usually did.

On the second morning we were there, Rosco came to seek me out. He put his arms around me and dropped a kiss on top of my head. He seemed to have forgotten all about the recent incident, although it seemed that when he was trying to ignore his bad behaviour, he was more affectionate to me.

'I have to beg a very big favour of you, *cara mia.*'

'Yes?' I said warily as I stepped out of his arms, but he came after me and held me close again.

'I have had a call from Davina, and there is a crisis at home. One of my suppliers has breached our contract, and I need to be there to sort it out. Would you be very unhappy if we left today?'

He didn't have to be Einstein to see how

unhappy I was here.

But I was torn. It would be nice to have some space. If I stayed here for a week, I could go to London and catch up with my friends.

And buy a bloody phone. I had managed to make a brief call to Sienna on the landline in the kitchen, and I knew I'd worried her as I'd fobbed her off. She had always been able to read me well.

If I was totally honest it would be nice to have some space from Rosco.

'How about you go back, and I'll follow in a few days. You're going to be busy.'

Wrong answer.

His fingers tightened on my upper arms and I tensed.

'No. You will come home with me. I have bought our tickets. We fly out of Gatwick at three o'clock this afternoon.'

I couldn't help myself. Maybe being in my home gave me courage. I shook his arms off and folded my arms. 'So, what was the point in asking me a favour? You have already decided what is happening.'

'Yes, that is correct. I am your husband.'

'So? Does that mean I have no say in any decisions we should make together?'

His dark eyes glittered with suppressed rage. Maybe knowing that my father was in the house bolstered my courage.

'I'm going to stay here. Change my ticket and I will follow you on the weekend. I haven't even seen my sisters yet.'

'We are being picked up at noon. Be ready.' He turned on his heel and left the room.

I sank onto the bed and put my face in my

hands
Was I strong enough to disobey him?
To my disgust I knew I wasn't.

We'd been back in Italy for three months, and Rosco's behaviour had improved. He hadn't been drinking much, and had been at several meetings in the city, leaving me to explore the villa. I still didn't have my own phone, but he often gave me his—and privacy—to call my friends. I was even allowed to go down to the village by myself some days. It had been thirteen weeks since we had left my parents' home. To my surprise, my father had called the villa the week after we got home and asked to speak to me.

'Dad? What's wrong?'

'Nothing,' he replied, his voice bright. 'Can't a father ring his daughter and say hello?'

I held back my cynical reply that I couldn't ever recall him ringing me before.

'I just wanted to call and see how you had settled in Italy. It's a big step, Marissa.'

I had a feeling that Dad had overheard our argument the day we left, but he never said anything specific.

'It is.'

Rosco was hovering.

'If you ever need anything don't you hesitate to call me.'

'Thank you, Dad. That's kind of you.'

'You just remember that we love you, chicken. No matter what you might think.'

My eyes had welled up at that. I'd forgotten the nickname Dad had had for me when I was a child.

I hung up the phone and went to walk out of the study.

'What was kind?' Rosco asked.

'Dad asked if we'd like to visit soon.'

'We will try.'

But of course, we didn't.

Sometimes a niggle of doubt crept in and I wondered if Rosco could somehow hear the calls I made on his phone, but I shook that suspicion off. I was getting paranoid. Sienna and I chatted at least once a week and I had become very skilled at sounding happy and prattling on about the villa and the countryside, but never anything about my marriage.

Rosco had asked me to redecorate one of the smaller guest rooms, and I soon discovered that his interpretation of the word was very different to mine. Beautiful timber panelling covered the far wall and needed resealing.

I was in my element. I found an old pair of shorts and a stained T-shirt deep in my luggage, and I went ferreting in the barn down behind the villa and discovered some tins of varnish. I had spent two peaceful days rubbing back the timber and resealing it. The smell of the old timber soothed me, and my fingers itched to build something.

My joy was short-lived. I heard Rosco's car roar up the long drive mid-afternoon on the second day, and Davina must have told him where I was because only moments later, he was at the bottom of the ladder I was perched on.

'What the hell are you doing?' His voice

was thunderous.

'I am doing what you asked me to. You said the guest bedroom needed redecorating.'

I climbed down the ladder and wiped a hand over my sweaty brow.

'You look like an *il lavoratrice.*'

'A lavatory?' I gaped at him. Something had gone astray in the translation.

'A labourer,' he said impatiently. 'I meant for you to choose the fabrics and the colours and order them online, not ruin your beautiful hands and nails scrubbing down walls.

I stared back. Hard.

'It might be that "lavatory" word, but that is my trade. I was a woods craftsman in London.'

'I don't care what you were in London, my wife will not work like a common labourer.'

I sighed and climbed down the ladder.

'Well, what can your wife do to fill in her days?'

He looked at me as though I had two heads.

'Be a wife.'

'Yes, Rosco,' I said with a bit of snark in my tone. 'I guess I can be a wife. But perhaps not to your satisfaction.' His disparagement of my profession had rankled. 'Perhaps we have different ideas of what a wife should be. Perhaps this isn't going to work.'

'What?' He screwed up his face. 'The room? I can get someone in to fix it.'

'No, our marriage. I think I need some time away.' I half turned away and I didn't see the blow coming.

The next thing I knew I was on the floor, my head hard up against the ladder and my left ear ringing like a church bell. He leaned over and grabbed my hair and pulled me up. Searing pain ripped through my scalp. He held me upright as he yelled into my face. My head was spinning but I could hear his words.

'You will not leave me. If you do, I will kill you. Is that clear? You took a holy vow, and you are my wife for the rest of your life.'

'What?' I whispered as shock flooded through me.

'If you don't believe me, think of Celeste. She too wanted to leave me.'

'Who is Celeste?' I whispered as I moved my tongue around my mouth. I had a feeling I had a loose tooth. My cheek was stinging and aching where I had hit the floor.

'Celeste was my wife, and she tried to leave. She met with an accident and I was heartbroken as I would be if you were to meet with an accident.'

Horror filled me as I stared at my husband, but his face disappeared as he pulled me close and my face was pressed into his linen shirt.

'My poor darling. How clumsy of you to fall off the ladder. Shall I get Davina to call the doctor?'

'No.' My voice was muffled against his shoulder as I fought tears. 'I will have a shower and lie down.'

'And you will be more careful next time.' His voice was full of sympathy. 'Although there will not be a next time, will there?'

'No, Rosco, there won't.' My voice was dull.

The diamond necklace and matching earrings that appeared on my dressing table the next week were obviously supposed to make me forget what he had done this time.

Chapter 16

Pippa: Pentecost Island

Eliza was sitting on the steps when I walked back through the gate.

'I was waiting to see what you had lined up for me today, Pippa.' Her smile was wide, but her eyes didn't quite meet mine.

I cut straight to the chase. 'What was all that about?'

'What?' she asked innocently. 'What was what about?'

'All that guff with Phillipe. You disappeared like a shot when he arrived yesterday, and you were off like a frightened rabbit when you saw him this morning.'

'I was doing the right thing. You had a guest and you surely didn't want the handy man hanging around.'

'Handy woman.' I sat on the step beside her. 'You are more than a worker, Eliza. You fit in so well with us all, I thought you would consider yourself a friend by now.'

'I'm sorry if I did the wrong thing.'

'Are you sure you don't know him? He said you reminded him of someone.'

'No, I don't know any Phillipe from France. A bit out of my league. A girl from a fishing family in little old EnZed. I've never been to France.' Her smile was rueful. 'Not the sort of circles I mix in.' She lowered her head. 'I am a bit shy too. I had a tough childhood, so I don't have a lot of confidence around people. I'll probably move on when you start getting guests here.'

'So, you're sure you don't know him? He said you looked like someone called Marissa. A sister? A cousin?'

'Nope.' She shook her head. 'I don't know anyone of that name.'

'Okay. Come on then. Let's get to work.'

'What's on the agenda for today?'

'I'd like to tell you about some ideas I've had for knocking some walls out in the house. And to see if you think it can be done.'

'Thank you,' she said quietly. 'You don't know how much it means to me, to have my opinion valued.'

'I've really taken on your idea of the spa too. I couldn't get to sleep last night thinking about it. I think it would be a fabulous drawcard. I was even thinking about building a lodge further into the bush so we could use the house for the restaurant, the spa and a sitting room for the guests. I know what it's like on a boat. If they came up for lunch or dinner, they might appreciate a space to relax in afterwards.'

'You've got some plans, that's for sure.'

'Can I just ask you one thing?' I said carefully.

Her eyes narrowed. 'Does it involve people?'

'No. It only involves you and trust.'

'Okay, ask away.'

'Will you promise me that if it does come time for you to leave that you'll tell us and just won't disappear into the night the way you arrived?'

She nodded.

I held up my pinkie and crooked it.

'Promise?'

She looked at me blankly.

I chuckled. 'It's a tradition that Tam and Nell and I started at school. Make a promise, crook fingers.'

She slowly lifted her left hand and for the first time I notice that her little finger was already crooked.

'It might be hard,' she said. 'But I'll do my best.'

'That's great. It's the most I can ask.' I looked at her finger as she lowered her hand. 'What did you do to your finger?'

'Jammed it in a door.' She didn't meet my eye again. 'And I was nowhere near a hospital, so the break had to heal by itself.'

After we'd looked at my ideas and Eliza came up with some great ideas to add to what I suggested, we went down to the huts. Each hut was small but had a sandy level verandah at the front covered with an overhang of the roof. The cladding I had ordered from the hardware store was a sandy colour and the huts with their straw-look roofs would blend into the beach.

'Have you thought about hanging some rope hammocks with coloured cushions on the verandah?'

I put my hands on my hips and regarded Eliza seriously. 'The day you decide to leave here is not going to be a good one. We might find some jobs for you out of the public view if that is what it will take to keep you here. Hammocks are a fabulous idea. See, I don't think of those things, although I do remember Nell imagining them between palm trees before we arrived. I'm into marketing, Tam is the foodie, Nell, the figures gal, and Evie, the landscaper. A side photo of the hut with a hammock looking out over the blue water of the bay would be a great shot for our brochure. I've been waiting for Rafe to come home to help me design it.'

'When does he come back?'

'Two more sleeps.' I grinned.

As we turned to head back up to the house, voices came from the bush.

Eliza froze. I glanced at her and put my hand on her arm. 'It's okay. It's only Evie and it sounds like Philippe.'

As we stood there, her hands went behind her back, and I could see them twisting nervously. She was tense and poised for flight and I wondered why she was so intimidated by strangers.

Evie's laugh preceded them as they stepped out of the rainforest.

'You didn't go climbing?' I addressed Philippe.

'No, Evie took me up as far as the beach to see Indian Head, but I'll leave it for a couple of days. I think that wind's going to come up today. Good for sailing but not so good when you are stuck on the top of a rock.' He looked at Eliza. 'Hello. I'm Phillipe Renton. I'm sorry I was rude this morning, but for a short time I thought you were someone else. Someone I used to know back in Europe.'

Eliza nodded. 'It's fine. I was rude too. I don't cope with strangers well.' She kept her hands behind her back, until Philippe held out his hand. She took his right hand with hers and they shook briefly.

'Eliza Pengelly. And I've never been to Europe,' she said.

Phillipe stared at her and she lifted her chin and stared right back.

Chapter 17

Marissa

The next twelve months was like living in a nightmare that I couldn't wake up from. I had no direct contact with my family or Sienna, as Rosco, and I travelled around the coast of Europe in his *Lady Calypso*. I was permitted to send a postcard every few weeks, but he scrutinised my message each time.

He was so clever, making sure no one was concerned about me or my whereabouts. No one knew of my real situation. As far as they knew I was having a wonderful life with my millionaire husband.

I should have been grateful that I was seeing so much of the world, but it was very hard to focus on the beauty and scenery around me when I was so tense. Occasionally we would have dinner with Ren, but most of the time it was just the two of us.

At least Davina was off the scene, but Rosco spent a lot of time on the phone to her, discussing business. Would you believe I still didn't know what his actual business was? The one time I asked all I got in response was a casual hand wave.

'Don't you worry your pretty little head about that, *cara mia*.'

Occasionally I was allowed to go into some of the small villages for shopping, but Rosco was always by my side, holding my hand and watching my every interaction, and doing the talking for me.

'You must learn to speak Italian.'

I had picked up a lot of the language, but I

kept that to myself.

I began to abhor his touch, even when he was telling me how much he loved me and held me gently. I found it difficult to eat and I knew I was losing weight. One thing I did do religiously, was take my contraceptive pill; if I was going to escape this monster—and yes, that is what he was—I couldn't afford to have a child with me when I finally got away.

He had now told me several times that if I left him, my life would be over; and I know he meant it literally. My days were filled with frustration and fear, and at times, I thought I was going to go crazy. But I was constantly seeking ways to get away.

I *would*.

And if I died in the attempt, it would be better than the life I was living with him

One day when we were moored off the Italian coast, I disagreed with Rosco about something minor. It was so inconsequential I can't even remember what it was now. He walked over to me with a grim smile.

'I don't like it when you are rude to me,' he said. He took my hand and slammed it in the cupboard in the galley. My little finger broke and I lived on painkillers for a week.

Of course, even though it had been deliberate, my husband was full of remorse. 'I am so sorry, Marissa, but you need to be more careful.'

'Yes, careful with who I pick to marry,' I thought cynically.

Careful about what I say. Careful about what I think. Careful about how I look at any man who may walk past or wave from another boat.

My finger hadn't healed when Ren joined us for dinner in the first little *taverna* we had visited on our honeymoon near the island of Mljet. I recalled Rosco's story of the man imprisoned on the island by the nymph and thought how our roles had been reversed. Is that why he had chosen that destination? I wondered.

Ren was as reserved as ever with me, but this time I saw him looking at me with concern. I had come to like him very much and I couldn't understand his friendship with Rosco. I loved listening to him talk; his views on life were very philosophical. His manner was always calm, and his voice was pleasant to listen to. Some nights, I would simply sit there and listen to the cadence of his voice, not hearing the words that he was speaking as he and Rosco spoke.

'You have lost weight, Marissa, and you are very quiet. Are you well?' he said as we waited for our meal. I had barely said a word since we had sat down.

Rosco interrupted before I could reply. 'We are hoping that a *bambino* is on the way. She has the morning sickness.'

Liar, I thought. We'd never even discussed that. *Thank God.*

'What did you do to your finger?' Ren asked looking at my bandaged pinkie.

'She jammed it in the cupboard in the galley. Silly girl.'

This time when Rosco replied for me, Ren raised his eyebrows and looked at me.

'Is it broken?'

I shrugged and an unspoken message passed between us. Luckily Mauro, the owner of the *taverna,* had come over to speak to Rosco and he didn't notice, or I would have paid for that too.

I could sense that Ren wanted to speak more to me, but Rosco didn't leave my side the whole evening.

He never did.

I felt sad as we waved Ren off early the next morning. Even though he was Rosco's friend he had always been kind to me.

'I won't see you both for a while. I am going to Australia.'

He hadn't mentioned that at dinner.

'*Bon voyage,*' I called.

He tipped his head and stood there looking at me until he was no longer in sight.

I felt bereft and turned with a sigh to go down and prepare Rosco's breakfast. I had finally learned to operate the stove in the galley and to cook.

As he sat there chewing a piece of toast, slowly and methodically—even that habit annoyed me now—Rosco slapped his hand on his thigh.

'Let's go to Australia too.'

'What?' I swallowed nervously. 'Sail *Lady Calypso* to the other side of the world?'

'No, don't be so stupid, Marissa. I will get my crew to take my motor cruiser there and when it has arrived, we will fly over.'

Three months later, we arrived in Australia, flying into Cairns International airport in the southern spring, eighteen months to the day after we had married. We made our way to the marina, and sure enough Rosco's super yacht was there. I had never seen this one before—she was called *Nymph*—but I was very pleased to see the vessel had a crew. A captain, a chef, and three deckhands, one of whom doubled as a hostess who serviced the rooms.

And more than that, as I was to discover.

The crew lined up—just like on a TV show about the rich and famous—and Rosco introduced them to me. 'This is my wife Marissa. Marissa, this crew has been on *Nymph* since I purchased her. They are loyal to me.'

Was it a hidden warning? Or was I completely paranoid?

Captain Sterling was an Englishman with silver hair and a cultured voice, but his eyes were cold. Jacques, the chef, was French, and had a nice smile. Dylan, Gareth and Rosa were the three deckhands. Of course, Rosa, an Italian, was very beautiful, and I noticed the way she fluttered her eyes at Rosco as she chattered away to him. Gareth seemed shy, and Dylan was Australian, a serious young man who shook my hand warmly.

It was wonderful to have other people around. Maybe Rosco would be more like the man I had married with others onboard.

'I'm very pleased to meet you all,' I said quietly, not sure how much I was supposed to say or interact with them, but Rosco beamed.

He was in a good mood, and that boded well for my peace of mind . . . and physical wellbeing.

We cruised north to the tip of Australia, and the weather was so hot, I spent most of my days in the air-conditioned saloon.

Rosco had words with me one night, but he didn't touch me, but he yelled so loudly I'm sure the crew would have heard his raised voice.

'You are letting yourself go, Marissa.'

I looked at him, surprised as he pointed angrily to a chip in my fingernail polish. 'I want perfection,' he screamed.

Dylan brought me a cup of tea up from the galley the next afternoon. Rosco was in the small office off the bridge on the floor above our cabin.

'I know you enjoy your cups of tea,' he said with a smile. 'Earl Grey, okay?'

'Thank you.' I took the tray from him and smiled back when I saw the two homemade biscuits on the tray. 'You are very kind.'

He looked nervous and lowered his voice. 'Madam, I hope I am not speaking out of turn . . .'

I raised my eyebrows as he glanced at the door.

'If you ever need anything, I can help.' With those enigmatic words he left, and I wondered what he meant. I wondered if Celeste had been on this boat before me, and they all knew what Rosco was like.

But I didn't trust anyone. For all I know Rosco could have put him up to it.

As the weeks passed, and we cruised to the Kimberley coast and back to Cairns, I learned to trust Dylan. He never spoke to me or looked at me in Rosco's presence, but we had many long conversations when Rosco was onshore conducting business in Cairns and Darwin or locked away in the office. One thing I did notice was Rosa's absence each time Rosco went ashore, or into his office, but I really didn't care. I guess I knew now I was merely an ornament for him. Hopefully, I might be replaced by the young Italian woman. That would be an easy out.

Dylan talked to me when I went up to the deck and told me about his life travelling around the world. One day he told me he would be leaving *Nymph* at the end of this voyage. He had secured another position on a boat in the Whitsunday Islands where he had grown up; his best friend from school was looking for a second skipper.

'Jiminy emailed me; he knew I wanted to come home. And that is home for me. I've seen enough of the world.'

'I'll miss your company and our talks,' I said, keeping an eye out for the taxi that would deliver Rosco back to the boat.

Dylan's brown eyes were intense as he looked at me. I was lying on a sun lounge on the upper deck and he was polishing the rail. Like everything else Rosco owned, the boat was expected to be gleaming and spotless at all times. Woe betide anyone who let a drop of water mar the shining surfaces.

'I find it a very difficult environment to work in. It's past time for me to leave,' he said. 'I'm going to leave *Nymph* when we return from Green Island. I know he'll be angry, but I'll give up a month's pay to get off.'

'Lucky you,' I muttered beneath my breath, but his hearing was acute.

'Forgive me if I am speaking out of turn, but why do you stay with him, Marissa? He treats you very badly.'

I shrugged. 'I have no choice.'

'You do, you know.'

I shook my head and Dylan put down the cleaning cloth and crouched beside me. 'Get off the boat at Cairns and fly back to England.'

Tears welled in my eyes. 'If only it was so easy, Dylan. You know yourself what he's like. He can't handle not being in control. I don't have any money, and I don't even have a phone.'

'Has he ever hurt you?' he asked softly.

I held up my left hand and showed him my crooked finger. 'He regrets it now as he says I am flawed. Rosa is now the one in his sights.'

'But you're his wife!'

'Trust me, I would do anything not to be. He told me if I ever leave, he will kill me. And I know he means it. His first wife died in an "accident".' My voice shook and I looked over to the terminal at the end of the wharf. Rosa and Rosco were walking on their way to the wharf where *Nymph* was moored. I could hear his laughter and her chatter from where I was sitting.

'They're on their way back.'

Dylan picked up the cloth and moved to the far end of the top deck. As he walked away, he looked at me. 'I have an idea.'

Two weeks later, Rosco decided we were

going to go to the outer reef.

'The snorkelling is very good at Green Island. I think you will enjoy it, Marissa,' he said as Gareth served our meal. 'We are leaving tomorrow.'

'Thank you, Rosco. I will enjoy that.' The correct responses came easily now. I was a fast learner. My only regret was that after we went to Green Island, Dylan—my only friend—would also leave the boat.

When Rosco disappeared into his office and I went up to the deck the next morning, Dylan sought me out, his eyes gleaming with excitement.

'I have a plan.'

I listened as he told me what he had done.

And smiled.

Everything was going to be all right. Or as right as my life could be from this point on, if I wanted to live.

Chapter 18

Pippa: Pentecost Island

The night before I went to the mainland to pick Rafe up from Airlie Beach was the longest in all the weeks we had been on the island. I was so excited, I couldn't sleep, and when I did my dreams were full of Rafe. The usual doubts flew in, and for some reason I thought about Darren and how gullible I'd been there.

I knew it wasn't about sex for Rafe . . . because we hadn't slept together. I'd insisted on a slow and steady build to our relationship. I'd been hurt too many times before.

What if he had changed his mind about me while he was back in his familiar territory?

Why would a famous author want to hook up with a damaged PR consultant?

I got up at dawn, made myself a coffee and talked sense to myself as I sat out on the verandah. I looked across our beautiful bay, past Philippe's old boat, and up the hill to Rafe's house.

I had to learn to trust.

The girls had taught me that, and I knew I could trust each of them. True, they all had their own issues, like I did and like Rafe did, but we all cared about and looked out for each other.

Even Eliza, now.

That was life, and we had the best life on Pentecost Island.

Rafe was flying into Proserpine and catching the bus into the marina where I would be waiting for him. I'd organised for Bunnings to deliver the cladding we needed to the marina at ten o'clock, and God love Jiminy, he had offered to bring his boat to share the load.

Eliza had been online and had ordered the fittings for the interior of the huts, and I think she was as excited about the huts as I was about Rafe coming home.

Phillipe had been helping Evie in the gardens, and everyone was keen to get the place looking good for the opening and Rafe's return. Evie had ordered supplies as well. The boats were going to be laden on the way back.

It was hard to believe we had been here for almost four months and summer and the cyclone season were ahead of us. The friendships I had now were the backbone of my life. Even Eliza had thawed more, and I had a feeling she might stay.

The progress we had made while Rafe was away was amazing, and I knew he would notice a huge difference. Eliza was chafing at the bit, keen to get the cladding on the huts and get the interiors finished.

Nell had sorted her software and backup issue and was quietly working away in the office, but we enticed her out the night before Rafe was due home to have another get together in the bar. I was so pleased at how it had turned out. Now we had to get the customers.

'Can we invite Phillipe?' Evie asked with a hopeful look. She had been trying hard to get his attention, but I don't think there was any interest on his part.

I shook my head. 'Let's make it a girls' night. We'll invite him tomorrow night when Rafe is home.'

Eliza sent me a grateful look. I know she still felt uncomfortable when Philippe was around, but I had seen them have a couple of brief conversations in passing.

Tam, Nell, Evie and Eliza and I had a pleasant night in the bar. Tam cracked a bottle of bubbles and we sat watching the mast lights come on as the sun set. There seemed to be a lot of yachts in the Passage and I hoped that they would come to our bar when it was open.

We talked—even Eliza It was one of those nights where everyone opened up, and we had a few "deep and meaningfuls".

'Of course, we won't see much of Pippa for the next few days.' Tam's grin was evil. 'There's a bit of catching up to be done there.'

Even Eliza smiled. 'Let her be. It's good to see someone happy.'

Evie leaned forward. 'What about you, Eliza? Anyone special on your horizon? Anyone at home in NZ?'

She shook her head but didn't say much. 'No. How about you, Evie?'

'I've had a couple of relationships, but both guys were ready to settle down, and I was keen to keep travelling. We parted on good terms, and I'm happy with the way things are for a while.'

'What about Phillipe?' Tam said. 'I thought you were interested.'

'He's a nice guy but a bit serious for me. Intense. He's got his eye on Eliza,' Evie said as she held up her glass. 'I've seen the way he looks at you. Very interested, I'd say.'

'He needn't waste his time,' Eliza said.

'He'll move on soon. He wanders the world.'

Nell frowned. 'How do you know where he's been. I didn't think you spoke to him much.'

Eliza flushed and waved her hand. 'I'm just assuming that by looking at his boat.'

'It's got character,' I said.

'I think Pippa's the only one destined for a happy ever after,' Tam said with a sigh as she opened the second bottle of bubbles.

I put my hand up. 'No more for me. I want a clear head tomorrow.'

'Aw, come on. You're no fun anymore.' The cork flew off with a loud pop and Tam laughed.

'If we keep doing this, we'll drink all the profits,' I replied, shaking my head. 'Won't we, Nell? All right, one more and then I'm off to bed.'

Rafe's flight was on time and I'd worked out almost to the minute how long it would be before the bus dropped him at Coral Sea Marina. I was waiting on the wooden benches underneath the big umbrellas near the roundabout when I saw the airport transfer bus come down the hill from the main road. I usually wore shorts and a T-shirt on the boat, but today I'd dug out one of my floral sundresses, and a straw hat.

I stood up as my heart picked up its pace, and a wonderful feeling of anticipation ran through me.

My gorgeous man was first off the bus, and my eyes drank him in as he looked over and saw me waiting. His gaze held mine and a slow smile spread across his face.

Rafe strode across and stood in front of me, his smile growing wider as he held my gaze.

'Hello there,' I said shyly.

'Hello, back. Oh, how I've missed you, Pippa.' He lifted both hands and cupped my cheeks gently, holding my gaze. He leaned forward until his lips met mine.

I lifted my arms and linked my hands behind his back revelling in his kiss that lasted for a very long time. Finally, we were interrupted by a call.

'Hoy, mate. Do ya want your bag or not?'

Rafe chuckled and pulled away. He turned to the bus driver and waved. 'Just leave it there please.'

'Whoa.' I fanned myself. 'I'm glad you don't go away too often.'

We walked over together to collect his suitcase, and I held onto his hand, not wanting to let him go.

'It's so good to have you back,' I said.

'It's good to be back. I told Jenny this is the last trip back there for a long time. Now that this promo model is set up, we can do the next one over the internet.'

'The next one? I'm pleased to hear that.

He nodded. 'Jack Smith signed another three-book deal with Jenny and Bryant.'

'You're going to be too busy for me, then.'

'Never,' he said dropping another kiss on my lips. 'But you might have to spend some nights up at my place.'

'Might I?' I said as I held his gaze.

We walked towards the wharf, and he looped his arm around my shoulder, the warmth of his body pressing against mine.

'How's everything back on the island?' he asked. 'And everyone?'

'I can't wait to show you what we've done. The bar is finished, but we delayed the opening until you came home. It looks fantastic and we've sort of already got our first guest moored in the bay. He's a Frenchman who knew Aunty Vi.'

'I can't wait to see it all.'

As we reached the wharf, Rafe paused and looked down at me.

'Have you had time to think while I've been away,' he asked quietly.

I nodded and tried to look serious. 'I have. I do have one question for you.'

Rafe's eyebrows rose and his brow crinkled in a frown. 'Is there something wrong?'

'Maybe.' I bit my lip. 'It all depends on you.'

'What do you want to know?'

My smile was wide as I reached up and touched his face. 'Can I have a sleepover at your place tonight?'

Chapter 19

Marissa: Great Barrier Reef

The voyage out to Green Island was rough, but I was almost shaking with excitement. I had to quell the anticipation that was zinging through me. I avoided any contact with Dylan as I couldn't trust myself not to smile, and I didn't want Rosco to notice anything different about my behaviour.

As Jacques served our dinner the night before we were due to arrive at the island, Rosco was particularly pleasant to me.

'Are you looking forward to snorkelling on the reef, *bella*?'

I looked down and nodded. 'I am. It will be good to get off the boat for a while.'

'You are sick of being on our beautiful boat,' he snapped as soon as Jacques went back to the galley. 'You are ungrateful for your good fortune.'

'I'm sorry, I meant it will be good to get in the water.'

That seemed to placate him, and he narrowed his eyes as he lifted his glass. 'Your cheeks are very flushed. You are not getting a flu, I hope.'

'No, it is just warm in here.' I said.

'Perhaps we should go to bed.' His eyes gleamed. 'It will be cooler in our cabin.'

'I would like to go and look at the stars on the deck with you.' I couldn't stand the thought of him touching me.

'Jacques, we shall have our dessert on the upper deck,' he informed the chef.

It was cool and windy on the deck and as I had hoped, Rosco was soon bored with the magnificent view of the stars, and with my company.

'I am going to work in my office for a while,' he said.

He stumbled on the way back to the stairs and I smiled. It was a rough night just as Dylan had said it would be. The wind whistled past the boat and the waves slapped noisily on the side as we ploughed through the swell.

I waited until Rosco had disappeared, and my hands shook as I hurried across to my usual sun lounge. I lifted the cushion and as Dylan had promised, there was a black stinger suit and inflatable PFD beneath the cushion. I carried them to the small deck at the back of the boat, sick with nerves, watching for the light that I had been told to wait for.

It was not the sea that was worrying me, it was the thought of my husband coming up and discovering me. I quickly pulled the suit on over my clothes, willing my hands and legs to stop shaking. I kept my shoes on and made my way to the ladder at the side of the deck. I slipped the flotation device over my head, then gripping the sides that were wet and gritty with salt, I climbed down to the second lowest rung of the ladder and waited.

He must have been watching. Not far from the left side of the boat, I saw a light flashing, and then the faint sound of a motor. I took a deep breath and stepped into my next life.

Chapter 20

Eliza: Pentecost Island

Knowing that Ren—or Phillipe as he seemed to be known now— was on the island stressed me out no end. I wondered whether to stay or go, but in the end, I figured he would eventually move on. As long as he knew me as Eliza, and he didn't know it was me, or what had happened, it would be fine. Rosco could never, never find out where or who I was now. If he did, well . . . I didn't want to think about it.

I also knew in the worst possible situation that Pip, Tam, Nell and Evie would support me. I would trust those girls with my life. I know Pippa had been slow to accept me, and I could understand that because I'd screwed up my story when my kayak had rolled, and I'd ended up almost drowning in front of their island. How ironic would that have been. As I'd come to, I know I'd made up names, and that Dylan, Alex and Marissa had rolled off my tongue.

Such a stupid mistake.

But Pippa had learned to trust me, and I admired her for that. She was a great boss, and I loved working here with the girls on the island. I didn't want to go.

But I couldn't risk Phillipe knowing, or anyone finding out who I was and telling Rosco I was here. I knew he would come after me.

Eliza Pengelly had come into being on a rough and windy night near Green Island when Marissa Bertolini had fallen overboard and drowned. There were only three people in the world who knew the truth and I was one of them.

I trusted the others implicitly, especially Dylan. I owed Dylan my life. He swore that his brother, Alex, on Green Island could be trusted too.

Jumping off the ladder into the waters of the Great Barrier Reef that night had been a shock, and my head had gone under the water briefly, before the flotation device had brought me to the surface. Within a minute, a small rubber duckie had pulled up alongside me, and two strong hands had pulled me over the side.

The noise of the wind and the sea had covered the small motor, and the darkness soon swallowed the bright lights of *Nymph* as Alex took me to safety.

I spent two weeks in total seclusion in a small two-room staff apartment on Green Island. Dylan's brother worked on the reef as a diving instructor and Dylan had organised my escape with him.

I had to stay inside until the fuss died down, but I didn't mind.

Two weeks after I had "drowned" there was a tap on the door of the apartment. Alex was out on a charter and I crossed the room hesitantly to stand at the door and listen, but I didn't speak or open the door.

'Marissa, it's okay. It's me, Dylan.' I opened the door and he held his arms open for a hug, and I fell into them.

I was shaking uncontrollably as reaction set in, and it took a good half hour and three cups of tea before I could speak calmly enough to thank him for what he had done. 'I owe you and Alex so much. How will I ever thank you?'

'By keeping safe, and not letting that bastard know you are alive.'

As we sat and drank endless cups of tea, we planned my return to the mainland.

'Have you left *Nymph* now?' I asked.

He nodded. 'Yes, it wasn't pretty. Even in his supposed grief, ten days after losing his wife, Rosco was able to call me every swear word that I've ever heard. English and Italian. Rosa and Gareth quit too. He is not happy.'

I shook my head, still unable to believe the generosity of Dylan—and his brother.

'It's over to you now, Eliza,' he said.

'Eliza?' I frowned.

'We went back to Cairns, and I was able to get you these.' He handed me a packet and I tipped it up. A black passport with a silver coat of arms on the front fell into my hand.

'Open it.'

I did as he bid, and stared at my face, but my long blonde hair had gone, replaced with dark curly hair cut short. My eyes dropped to the text below.

Eliza Pengelly, current address-Brisbane, Queensland.

'A passport! How did you do that?' I whispered. 'Where did you get it?'

'I have some very clever friends. That's all you need to know. What you need to do now, is cut your hair and dye it black.'

'I've been bleaching my hair since I was eighteen, 'I said. 'That photo is close to my natural colour.'

Dylan reached into the bag that he'd put on the floor. 'Until it grows out then . . . ta da!' He held out a packet of black hair dye.

Tears choked my throat and I put my hands over my face. 'How can I ever thank you?'

He rubbed my back gently. 'By becoming Eliza and staying safe. You realise that you can't let anyone know you are alive. Not your family or your friends? Not for a very long time anyway.'

'Could I go to the police? Tell them about Rosco?'

He shook his head. 'Do you think they would believe you? Has he broken the law? We know what he is like, but he is very clever. Did anyone ever see how he treated you?

I shook my head again. 'No.'

'Once we get you across to the mainland, I'm going to take you down to the Whitsunday Islands. There are thousands of backpackers down there, and a very casual employment system. You'll be able to find somewhere to live, and somewhere to work. Get yourself settled. We'll get you a kayak and I'll teach you how to get around. It would be wise to stay off public ferries and the like for a while.' He reached into his bag and pulled out a plastic bag. 'There's some money here to start you off. It should keep you going for a few months.'

'I will pay you back every cent,' I swore fiercely as I looked at the roll of bank notes.

'There's no need. I was very well paid on *Nymph*. Your—I mean Rosco—expected quality service, and he paid double the going rate.'

'Are you sure he believes I'm dead?' Uncertainty filled me, and I began to feel sick.

Could I do this? Take on a whole new identity and a new past? And not have any contact with my family? Could I start again?

Dylan reached into his bag and pulled out a newspaper. 'I knew you'd need reassurance. This is the *Cairns Post* from last weekend.'

My photo stared back at me, the headline announcing ***Italian Millionaire's Wife Pronounced Dead.***

Oh God. My family. My friends. Sienna.

They all thought I was dead.

But most important of all, so did Rosco Bertolini.

Chapter 21

Eliza: Pentecost Island

Pippa arrived home with a boatload of supplies, accompanied by a second boat skippered by her friend, Jiminy, and with Rafe. I said hello to them briefly, but I was more interested in the supplies on the boats.

'I'll help you get unloaded, Jiminy,' Rafe said with a yawn, but Pippa shook her head.

'No, love,' she said. 'You look tired. Go up to your place and I'll come up later.'

I felt sorry for Rafe when I saw the look on his face.

'We'll be fine. There's nothing heavy, you go up with Rafe,' I offered.

Evie came through the forest and waved to me. 'I'll give you a hand, Eliza.'

Evie was pleased because there were a few dozen tubes of starter shrubs that she'd ordered for gardens around the huts.

Jiminy's boat was unloaded first and we soon had a pile of building materials next to the huts.

'Oh. Look at these,' Evie exclaimed as she found the box of shrubs on Pippa's launch.

I walked along the wharf on the way back from unloading the boxes of squares that would clad the huts. As I looked up Phillipe walked out of the rainforest, a knapsack on his back, and a water bottle swinging from his hand.

'How was it?' Evie called out from the wharf. 'Did you get to the summit?'

'I did,' he called back. I'll just throw these on my boat, and I'll help you.'

'We're fine, almost done,' I said without looking at him. The less time I spent in Phillipe's company the better.

He ignored my comment, and soon returned and helped Jiminy unload the last boxes of cladding. I muttered under my breath as I finished off the load on Pippa's boat and Evie looked at me curiously. 'Calm down, girl. He's only trying to help.'

'I know.'

'And he's a nice guy.'

'I know that too,' I muttered again.

'So, what's your problem?' she persisted.

'I don't have one.'

Evie stood there with her hands on her hips. 'Sure looks like it to me. And Pippa won't be happy with you being rude to the guests.'

'I wasn't being rude,' I said in a low voice. 'And Pippa won't want the guests working on the island. What if he hurt himself? He wouldn't be covered by insurance.'

When we were done, Phillipe disappeared and Jiminy motored out of the bay and headed back to Hamo.

I grinned as he waved. I was feeling accepted and even starting to think like a local.

The next day I started work lining the exterior of the huts. It was a simple job as the cladding came in squares that I could manage. It only took me an hour to get the first hut finished. I slowly stepped backwards towards the rainforest keeping my eye on the angles and the joins to check it was all square. I nodded with satisfaction as I took the last step back and let out my breath as I walked backwards into someone.

'Oh, sorry,' I said turning around and held my breath as I looked up into an intense dark gaze. Of course, it had to be Ren.

Phillipe, I corrected myself silently.

He stared at me for a long moment, his gaze raking my face. He reached up and smoothed his finger along my eyebrow. 'Do you know you have the most unusual eyebrows?' he said softly.

'What?' I said.

'I noticed them the very first time I saw you when you came up on the deck wearing that colourful sarong.'

I took a step back as dread pooled in my stomach. 'I don't know what you're talking about.'

'I was horrified to see that Rosco had a new wife, and it didn't take me long to figure out that you knew nothing about Celeste.'

I tried to speak but the words wouldn't come as my throat closed.

'I didn't know what to do or say. I knew what Rosco could be like, but he seemed to be treating you well.' His voice surrounded me, and I felt faint.

I backed away further and my ankle twisted on a log as Ren followed me into the dimness of the rainforest. The only sound was my laboured breathing and the swish of leaves as the gentle morning breeze blew in from the bay.

'No,' I finally managed to say.

'I made sure I knew where you were sailing, and I followed you as much as I could without Rosco getting suspicious. I couldn't tell you that I knew what he could be like, in case he was different with you.' He reached for my left hand and held it up. 'But when I saw your broken finger, I knew.'

I choked on a sob. 'Please, please don't tell him where I am.' My hands were shaking, and silver lights began to prick at my vision. Just when I thought I was safe, he had to come to our island. My knees were trembling so much I slid down onto the bed of dead leaves that littered the floor of the forest.

'Marissa . . . Eliza.' Ren crouched down beside me. 'It's all right now. Everything is going to be all right.'

I put my hands to my face as his arm went around my shoulders. As much as I was scared of what was going to happen, his touch calmed me.

'You don't know what has happened? How long have you been on this island? How did you get here?' His questions tumbled one after the other as I moved my hands and turned my face into his neck. His skin was smooth and smelled of the sea. 'When I thought you had drowned, I was sick with guilt. I blamed myself. If I had interfered and stopped Rosco—'

I lifted my head and looked at him. Calm and gentle eyes held mine. 'You won't tell him, will you?' I whispered.

'I can't tell him, *mon ange.*'

'Thank you.'

'*Non.*' He shook his head. 'I cannot tell him because Rosco is dead.'

I widened my eyes and my breath caught. 'What? How can he be dead?'

'You do not read the news here?'

'No. Are you sure?' I lifted my hands and tugged at the front of his shirt. 'Or are you tricking me? Did he send you after me?' My voice was shrill, and I started to cry in great choking sobs.

'Marissa—'

'Eliza?' Pippa and Rafe were hurrying along the path towards us. 'Are you all right? What's happened.' Pippa's voice was full of concern.

Ren stood and put his hand up. 'She is fine. Can you both wait with us while I tell her one thing, please?' He took my hands and helped me to my feet and kept hold of me.

'Rosco's boat was hit by a container ship as it headed north of Cairns about three weeks ago. There were only two on board, Rosco and the skipper. For some reason they did not show up on radar. The boat was destroyed.'

'Are you sure? It's not a trick?' My voice was hoarse from crying.

'No, Marissa. Both bodies were recovered.'

The last thing I saw before I fainted into Ren's arms was Pippa stepping towards me.

Chapter 22

Marissa: Pentecost Island

Ren was flying back to England with me. He had called my parents and spoken to them first, so the call from me wouldn't be too much of a shock. Hearing my dad cry on the phone, saying, 'oh chicken,' over and over again brought me to tears. Even Mum had a bit of a weep. I'd been crying a lot these past few days too.

I'll never forget the call I made to Sienna that night. I cried and she screamed and sobbed over the phone.

'I'm coming home for a while in a couple of weeks,' I said. 'We'll come to see you.'

'We?'

'I have a friend who is coming with me.'

Dylan was over on Hamilton Island, I called him, and he came over the next morning. Knowing that *Nymph* had been destroyed and Captain Sterling and Rosco hadn't survived, shook him up. He put his arms around me and rested his forehead against mine.

'I thought I'd taught you better kayaking skills than that. You were supposed to paddle into the beach and say you'd heard that there might be some work going here. Not try and drown yourself around the point, girl!' He looked over at Pippa. 'I remember you from high school, and Jiminy is singing your praises about what you're doing over here.'

Pippa and Rafe, and the girls, wanted me to go home straight away to see my family, but they already knew I was alive and safe, and I insisted on finishing the four huts. Exteriors and interiors, and then staying for the opening of the bar. Ren did not leave my side for the whole two weeks as I worked. He was an excellent labourer.

The night that the bar opened the bay was full of boats. Ren had been out and put channel markers along each side of the channel and fifteen boats were tied to palm trees along the sand.

Pippa looked gorgeous as she greeted each of the guests. She was dressed in a pretty pink dress and Tam and Nell had burst out laughing when she walked into the bar before everyone arrived.

I frowned. 'What's wrong?'

Ren was beside me and looked at Pippa. 'You look very lovely. I cannot see why it is funny.'

Tam held her sides. 'Oh, Pip. You are completely in control now, aren't you? Pretty in pink of all colours!'

Rafe was beside her and Nell gave an unusual cheeky grin. 'All we want to know is if you have a pink G string too.'

Rafe and Evie looked confused, but Pippa, Nell, and Tam were almost in hysterics.

'We'll tell you the pink story after a few drinks,' Pippa said wiping the tears of laughter from her eyes. 'Now look, my mascara's run.' She took a breath and looked around at us all. 'Before everyone comes up from the boats, I want to say a few words.'

She took a deep breath. 'I want you to know how much I love you all.' She nodded at Ren too. 'Yes, Phillipe, Ren or whoever you are, you too. You've also been a fabulous help getting these huts ready these last few weeks.' She gripped Rafe's hand. 'Rafe, I want you to know how much I love you. You, my darling, are the love of my life.'

Rafe held her close and as they kissed, I wasn't ashamed to say that I blinked away tears.

Love could be real, and I had to learn to trust again. Ren was slowly helping me do that.

Pippa held her hands out and Rafe and Ren stood back as she got Tam, Nell, Evie and I to form a circle with her.

'You girls are the best friends a girl could ask for. You support me, you've helped me through the good and bad times, but most of all you have all worked your butts off to get Ma Carmichael's ready to open. I just want to thank you all before the party starts.' Pip turned to me. 'Eliza, one of the best things about the last few days was hearing that you and Phillipe are going to come back to the island after you go home. There will be a place here for both of you for as long as you want.'

We stepped out of Pippa's circle and soon the popping of champagne corks was the only sound. Ren touched my shoulder lightly and smiled down at me as he passed me a glass. A moment later, he held his glass to mine.

'To new beginnings, Eliza?'

I smiled at this gentle man. 'To new beginnings, Phillipe.'

When his lips brushed mine, I knew I was healing.

Epilogue

Nell: Hydeaway Bay-50 kilometres north of Airlie Beach

The forecast had been for a late storm, and for once, the weather bureau had been spot on. Nell O'Leary leaned forward, her attention focused on the road ahead, as the clouds grew darker and the wind whipped the low hanging branches of the trees into a frenzy. She clutched the steering wheel harder as the dirt road petered to a track.

Surely this couldn't be the right road?

The address for *ND IT Services* had read 655 Dingo Beach Road, Hydeaway Bay, and the signpost about five kilometres back had confirmed that she had taken the correct turn when she'd pulled over and checked her phone.

She was on the right road—although it was more a track—and she was determined to find the blasted place.

Frustration vied with anger, and she considered turning around, but the track was so narrow it would take about a ten-point turn to go back the way she'd come.

Besides she *had* to see this guy. She'd had no luck in Proserpine at the computer store and the technician there had sent her fifty kilometres north to Hydeaway Bay, where he had assured her there was a networking guru who would go out to Pentecost Island and solve her problem. But it was heading for five o'clock and she was worried the company would be closed when she got there.

She'd tried to call, but the phone had gone to voicemail. She'd left a message, with her name and a quick outline of the problem, so at least they knew she was on her way.

Finally, a gate appeared ahead and in the fading light she could just read the number 655.

'Thank God,' she muttered under her breath. This was her last chance; if this guy couldn't help her, the opening of the resort was at risk. It was too late to get someone to fly up from the city and look at the problem; their opening was less than a week away, and she just couldn't let Pippa down.

The gate was closed, and Nell pulled over to the side of the road. The track was so narrow, another car couldn't get past her anyway. She grabbed her laptop and climbed out of the car.

With a frown, she looked ahead as she swung the gate open, again doubting that she had the right place.

'I've come this far, I might as well keep going,' she muttered.

Sure enough, a timber sign on the small dwelling ahead read *ND IT Services*, and Nell puffed out a sigh of relief. It wasn't an office, but a private house. A light was shining in the front window and she set off looking nervously at the long grass that was brushing her legs below where her shorts ended.

Please, no snakes.

A flash of lightning followed immediately by a huge crack of thunder that shook the ground, had her running fast through the long grass towards the two steps at the front of the house.

Nell stepped up onto the verandah and raised her hand to knock, but the door swung open before her knuckles reached the timber.

With a gasp, she took a hurried step back, but a hand shot out to grab her arm before she could fall backwards down the steps.

'Careful, sweetheart. I don't have any public liability insurance.'

Her heart thumped hard and she stared into the eyes of the man who had once made a fool of her. It might have been a long time ago, but she had never forgotten or forgiven him.

'Nat Dwyer, what the bloody hell are you doing here?'

'I could ask you the same thing, Nellie.'

Come and spend some more time with the girls on Pentecost Island...see if Eliza and Phillipe stay on the island. And Nell? Well . . .

Nell O'Leary sees the world in a logical way, and she's content managing her friend, Pippa's eco-resort. Despite her outgoing personality, she is painfully insecure around the opposite sex, and knows she is not a good PR face for the resort. When she runs into a technical problem, she hires an ex-colleague to help her sort it out.

Nathaniel Dwyer might be a computer whiz, but that's the only thing he and Nell have in common.

Nat is a womaniser—with no intention of ever settling down; he has worked too hard to keep his heart safe.

When Nell asks him to help out, he is happy to help. The last thing Nat expects is to fall in love with this quiet woman.

Nell falls hard and fast, but there is no way she would ever trust Nat.

Can they both overcome this lack of trust or is their past destined to cause them heartache?

OTHER BOOKS from ANNIE

Whitsunday Dawn
Undara
Osprey Reef
East of Alice
Porter Sisters Series
Kakadu Sunset
Daintree
Diamond Sky
Hidden Valley
Larapinta
Kakadu Dawn

Pentecost Island Series
Pippa
Eliza
Nell
Tamsin
Evie
Cherry
Odessa
Sienna
Tess
Isla

The Augathella Girls Series
Outback Roads
Outback Sky
Outback Escape
Outback Wind
Outback Dawn
Outback Moonlight
Outback Dust
Outback Hope

Sunshine Coast Series
Waiting for Ana
The Trouble with Jack
Healing His Heart
Sunshine Coast Boxed Set

The Richards Brothers Series
The Trouble with Paradise
Marry in Haste
Outback Sunrise
Richards Brothers Boxed Set

Bondi Beach Love Series
Beach House
Beach Music
Beach Walk
Beach Dreams
The House on the Hill

Second Chance Bay Series
Her Outback Playboy
Her Outback Protector
Her Outback Haven
Her Outback Paradise
The McDougalls of Second Chance Bay Boxed Set

Love Across Time Series
Come Back to Me
Follow Me
Finding Home
The Threads that Bind

Bindarra Creek
Worth the Wait
Full Circle
Secrets of River Cottage
Four Seasons Short and Sweet
Ten Days in Paradise
Follow the Sun
Others
Deadly Secrets
Adventures in Time
Silver Valley Witch
The Emerald Necklace
Christmas with the Boss
Her Christmas Star
An Aussie Christmas Duo (two Christmas novellas)
Bindarra Creek Duo

Acknowledgements

A special thank you to my wonderful editor and critique partner, Susanne Bellamy, and my eagle-eyed proof-reader, Roby Aiken.

About the Author

Author of the Year Ausrom Readers' Choice 2014

Best Established Author Ausrom Readers' Choice 2015

Finalist for Author of the Year, Book of the Year, Cover of the Year, Ausrom Readers' Choice 2016

Best Established Author, Ausrom Readers' Choice 2017

Book of the Year (Whitsunday Dawn) Ausrom Readers' Choice Awards 2018

Annie lives in Australia, on the beautiful north coast of New South Wales. She sits in her writing chair and looks out over the tranquil Pacific Ocean. She has fulfilled her lifelong dream of becoming an author and is producing books at a prolific rate.

She writes contemporary romance and loves telling the stories that always have a happily ever after. She lives with her very own hero of many years and they share their home with Toby, the naughtiest dog in the universe, and Barney, the rag doll kitten, who hides when the grandchildren come to visit.

Stay up to date with her latest releases at her website: http://www.annieseaton.net

If you would like to stay up to date with Annie's releases, subscribe to her newsletter on her website.